GRETCHEN'S SURPRISE

STEPHANIE BOYER

Chapter One

She took a long pull off of her Landshark Lager. The cool beer always went down smoothly; with a frown she thought of her husband, well, ex-husband, who always drank her beer out of the fridge. I guess after spending fifteen years with someone there were things that brought back memories. But, Gretchen Mitchell was determined to be a new woman with a new life.

She was a newly divorced thirty-five year old woman who worked as a nurse to pay her bills. Since she was born and reared in rural Missouri, her country roots taught and expected her to get married and have a baby so she did. From the outside, Gretchen's life was model perfect with a husband and son. Nothing like keeping the status quo, but it was oh so monotonous. She was a woman that needed a little spark in her life.

She looked around Silky's bar for Cherie and Lou, her two best friends. They all had decided to come to New Orleans for Mardi Gras to get away for a girls weekend. Her friends thought she needed a break and so they packed up and gassed up and left town the night before at 8 o'clock. They talked and laughed like close girl friends do about everything from the coolest shoes to the most erotic book they've ever read.

Gretchen located Lou with Sam, her latest fling. He reminded Lou of Evanovich's Ranger character in the numbers novels. Lou had a mild obsession with the character; truth be known, so did Gretchen. Who wouldn't want a mysterious bad boy? Sam was Cuban, reserved and had influence and power. Lou was a tall brunette with legs that reached from her armpits to the floor; she also had big blue eyes with Texas sized lashes. Her wit was biting and absolutely hilarious. Her brains intimidated many a man.

Cherie waved to her as she gladly followed a talk, dark and handsome on the dance floor. Cherie was on the dance team in college and could still bust a move. She didn't have to worry about not having a partner-on the dance floor or in her bed- with her slim, curvy body that could twist and tantalize. Men wanted to spend time with her friends; always the bridesmaid, never the bride kind of feeling crept over her.

Gretchen sighed and thought out loud, "One of these days." Although her southern accent was prominent, it didn't roll off the tongue like the Cajun French dialect from New Orleans. She leaned back against the bar to watch her friends; she loved the way her shirt slipped up at her waist to show a little bit of her flatter stomach from the hours she had spent at the gym.

Grey knew the Red Head didn't realize he was within earshot. He saw her walk in with her friends. This one didn't look like the usual barhopping type. He'd been here at Silky's Bar before and she wasn't a regular. Something about her was different than other women who had piqued his interest.

Her skin was slightly tanned and her hair was shiny auburn. She was about 5'6", curvy body with meat on her bones. She was wearing flip-flops, a denim short skirt on her perfectly rounded ass, and a snug, baby tee that covered her full breasts nicely, but would look much better on the floor of his hotel room. When she got closer and leaned against the bar, he noticed her toenails were painted hot pink. His weakness was pedicured bare feet with painted toenails. There was no way brains went with that total package. He slid over closer to her at the bar and asked, "One of these days, what?"

Gretchen gave a start when she heard the deep voice and turned to see solid muscle under the soft blue t-shirt. He stood with his arms crossed over his chest. His arms were pipes really; the muscles were so large and obviously defined even through the shirt. Those were arms of physical labor. Slowly she raised her eyes to meet his face.

On his square jaw, he wore a five o'clock shadow better than the swing on her Grandma's front porch. His lips were full and red, and he had green eyes like the Caribbean Sea, her favorite place. His wavy brown hair hung just a little over his bronze forehead and was long enough in the back to curl up his broad neck-one that really needed her lips on it. He looked to be the strong, silent type and quite delicious. Probably a Navy SEAL and so not her type, if she even had a type.

"I'm sorry?" Gretchen addressed the mystery man.

"You said, 'One of these days' and I was wondering what you meant," Greyson Maddock studied the woman as he answered.

"Oh, I didn't meant to speak out loud. I was just commenting on my friends and how carefree and happy they are. I was thinking I am going to be there one of these days." Gretchen paused. When she tilted her head to the side to examine him, her hair fell across her cheek and she smiled at him. "Why am I telling you this? You are a total stranger." Good grief, the man was smokin' hot and he was talking to her! Gretchen's ramblings sounded less than suave.

Mr. Mystery Man looked into his drink and slid a sideways glance her way. His one-sided smile warmed his face and his expression was more like a normal guy than a mercenary. "Hi, I'm Grey. I'm on my way to being carefree and happy." He raised his glass and his eyebrows to her and took a sip.

Gretchen looked at her new acquaintance. With a coy smile she replied, "Hi, I'm Gretchen." Just looking at him made her body blossom.

"Gretchen. Nice name to go with a sexy woman." Gretchen grinned at him like a silly schoolgirl. *Did this majorly hot man just say she was sexy? Oh. My. Gosh!*

"So, are you here with someone, Gretchen?" Grey needed to know if Mr. Muscles was going to come out of the restroom and pound on his head for talking to his woman at the bar. He had been there and done that and didn't like those travel plans.

"Well, Grey, I am with some friends, divorced and here to forget all about it. And you?" Gretchen hoped he accepted that answer. She didn't want to spend the evening talking about her failed marriage.

"Me? Uh, no, not married or engaged or otherwise entrapped; I have been married once at an early age. I'm too busy for all the responsibilities of a serious relationship." Greyson hoped he didn't sound crass, but it was the truth. He knew what it would take to be in a strong, healthy relationship with a woman and he was just not ready.

"I'm here doing some work on a project in town and it's really not going according to plan. I thought I might get some relief in a drink." Grey shrugged and smiled. He turned to her. "Conversation with someone that is easy on the eyes is even better." His eyes drifted lower to her mouth.

Whoa baby. "Hey, I'm sorry it's not working out. My life is too planned to the point of boring at times. So, tell me about the project that leaves you to seek relief with liquid that comes in a purple velvet bag?" Gretchen liked talking to this guy.

Grey laughed and the sound made her stomach do funny things. "Oh, I'm working on an abandoned ship. My company has been hired to sink it as a diving training site."

"Really? That's interesting. I like diving, although I've only done it a couple of times." With a frown, Gretchen continued, "How could it be stressful to sink a ship? I can demolish things really well. The problems begin when I try to put it back together."

Grey nodded and smiled. "It's really amazing, all the permits to request and red tape to wade through to do a job like this one. I've sunk a ship in the Caribbean with no problem. But in New Orleans it's a different story."

Gretchen rolled her eyes and took a sip of her beer. "Everything in New Orleans is a different story." She nodded and continued. "I've been to the Caribbean a couple of times and I loved it. I think I could be a beach bum for the rest of my life if I didn't have a child back home that needed his momma. In fact, come to think of it, I actually dove on a site off of St. Barts in the French West Indies this past October."

"No kidding? GMS, Incorporated sunk the one you dove on. My parents started the company. My mother and I run it now from the island. That was my favorite job. I was at home with that project." His face softened. Gretchen couldn't help but think that Grey probably had some hot moments in the sun with one of the islanders or its tourists and her face flushed. He was a very attractive, sexy man that women couldn't ignore. It also explained the great tan in the middle of February.

"Seems you found a way to relax in the Caribbean." She smiled lazily at him. Gretchen lipped her beer bottle and realized she had a pleasant buzz. It was very relaxing and felt wonderful.

Grey leaned into her, tilted his head so that his mouth almost touched the sensitive skin of her neck. When he spoke, Grey's voice was low and warm as his breath tickled her ear. "I can think of several ways I like to relax." Grey was surprised at the way this stranger's seductive scent affected his libido. She smelled so sexy.

Oh my gosh. Is he trying to pick me up? Gretchen thought of all the ways she wanted Grey-in her bed, on the bar, over the bar. It was an over-active imagination on her part. Mr. Hottie couldn't be coming onto her; her almost non-existent self-esteem was straining to keep up. Either way it went, he was making her hot. She took another drink of her beer for courage and decided to play the game if she could remember how it went.

Then, Gretchen leaned into him, looked into his green eyes and responded with, "Oh, yeah? Well, I'm sure it is pumping iron or running ten miles or something for you." Her eyes drifted to his chest and arms. For good measure she reached over and squeezed the large firm muscle bulging from under the sleeve of his t-shirt.

Grey looked down at her with heat in his eyes. He put the straw from his drink in the side of his mouth and said, "Well, darlin', it's physical, but running and lifting aren't what I had in mind." He turned and leaned back against the bar. The guy had a small diamond stud in his left ear. Yum. Her own Caribbean pirate.

He was damn sexy working the straw between his perfectly straight, white teeth and a lopsided grin on his face. Gretchen could picture him in nothing but his low-slung jeans, barefooted and looking at her; her insides went to mush. She had to bite her bottom lip to suppress a moan. If his arms were any indication of what the rest of his body looked like, it would be like Adonis. Her head was saying-better think about this. Her body was saying-yes, *yes*, YES! Her mouth said, "What do you have in mind?"

Chapter Two

He grinned and asked, "Wanna get out of here?" Gretchen nodded and put her empty beer down on the bar. Grey ordered two drinks to go while Gretchen checked in, or out really, with her friends. Grey liked watching her go; he liked the way her firm backside moved side to side as she made her way through the clutter of tables and people.

Gretchen arrived at Lou's table and let her and Cherie know that she was leaving with the guy at the bar. Lou said, "Girl! He is hot. You go and have a good time. You've got your cell and we know people here." Fortunately, Lou's new beau was a prosecuting attorney for the New Orleans parish. "Cherie and I will be back at the hotel at some point. Check in with us later." Lou was a big part of the reason Gretchen didn't lose her sanity when she split with her long-time husband and high school sweetheart. She cherished their friendship and she appreciated Lou's non-judgmental mind-set.

"Ok. I will call you." Gretchen hugged her friend.

"Be safe and do have fun. Do you still have your SIG?" Gretchen rolled her eyes but pointed to her purse in answer and Lou grinned, shook her head and waved her off. She turned back to Sam and said, "Hey, you've let my drink go empty. Shame on you." Gretchen smiled and shook her head. Sam was crazy about Lou and wanted something long term, but Lou was in it for the companionship in small spurts of time.

Gretchen grabbed her purse and waved to Cherie who was currently dancing with yet another perfect looking guy. Her husband trusted her to be faithful to their marriage vows when she was out with Lou and Gretchen. He also knew she would be dancing with anyone who would dance with her. He had always told her he didn't care who started her motor as long as she parked her car in his garage. Lucky woman, that one. Gretchen motioned that she was leaving with Grey and Cherie nodded and gave her a huge grin. She made the phone sign with her thumb to her ear and pinky to her mouth and lipped 'call me.' Cherie swirled back onto the dance floor. Nothing like a little bump and grind with some 'strange' in a public place.

Cherie, Lou and Gretchen were in town for the festivities. They decided after Gretchen's divorce to head down south for Mardi Gras. Gretchen was more of the reserved, cautious type. Gretchen thought this major swing in entertainment choices might send her off on an adventure to discover a new life. What could it hurt? She had a couple of friends who were game for just about anything.

Grey opened the door and the thickness of the New Orleans air hit them in the face. Even for February the temperature was very mild, but the humidity was a constant. The music faded the farther they walked from the bar. Bourbon Street was busy even for a Thursday night. Most of the people were coming in for Mardi Gras and so the party was non-stop no matter where you were. People were dancing and laughing and singing in the streets. Some were doing more than dancing and laughing and singing in the streets. It was just the sort of atmosphere that Gretchen needed to help get her mind off her divorce.

It had been several years since she was down south. She had come one time with a group of girlfriends. She had also been here with Jacob. She thought she would be with him forever. But, she decided after a child and many years of marriage that she couldn't live without the emotional side of a relationship and being second best to his true love-the store.

Gretchen was a woman who needed more than he was able and willing to give. Jake was a good man who never should have married and had a child. His family business was his passion. He had their child Jeb with him now in Missouri and was a good father for short periods when his work didn't interfere. That's the kind of husband he was, too; he was a good husband when the store was all under control-inventory counted and stocked up, which seemed to be nearly never.

Jake's family store was his number one priority and Gretchen couldn't continue to sacrifice her emotional health anymore. Oh, she had tried lots of things. Drinking. Walking. Painting. Getting a dog. Drinking. Reading. Taking anti-depressants. Changing jobs. Drinking. Nothing she did made her feel any better about their relationship; she really thought it was her since Jakob didn't feel like anything was wrong. Jake didn't seem to notice that she had slowly slipped away from him and the thing that hurt the most was that he didn't seem to care; he hadn't been invested enough in the relationship to realize something wasn't right. She had loved him heart and soul and made many decisions in her life based on what Jacob would like or where he wanted to live. She never should have made him the key to her happiness. Her mistake. Well, not anymore. Grey was not a choice that Jake would have made for her, that's for sure.

Grey reached over and laced his strong fingers between hers. He began to rub circles with his thumb around her thumb while looking at her. The crowd had thinned while they walked in silence. Soon they were at the river. Gretchen liked his touch and thought about his able fingers working on her body in other places.

"So, we've walked all this way and you haven't said a word. Have you changed your mind about leaving with me? If you want to go back, then I will take you. It sounds old-fashioned, but I am a gentleman." Grey seemed sincere in what he said.

"No, no I don't want to go back. Just a little preoccupied with my thoughts." Gretchen knew she had to get control of her thoughts. She didn't want to spend the rest of the evening with Grey and thinking about Jake.

"Give me a chance to make you forget whatever it is you are thinking about." Grey wrapped his arms around her and pulled her to his strong body; she felt his firm chest as her breasts mashed into him. He couldn't wait any longer to taste her lips. He wasn't as tall as Gretchen first thought and she barely had to reach up when his mouth came down on hers.

The kiss started out soft and slow. When she opened her lips, his tongue explored her mouth and licked the insides of her lips. Their tongues touched and tested, and then intertwined. She tasted a hint of Crown Royal in his kiss and heat shot to the important parts of her body. If just kissing him did this, then she was in trouble. He moaned and ended the kiss by gently sucking her lower lip into his mouth.

Grey looked at her with very smoky eyes. "I want you to know that I don't usually do this sort of thing." He leaned in and nibbled on an earlobe and then drew back to look at her. Gretchen thought she could possibly be the luckiest woman on the planet right now.

"Uh huh. I bet you say that to all the girls." She smiled and licked her lips.

"I wouldn't do that if I were you." Grey said. His green eyes were smoky and half lidded.

"Do what?" Her eyes grew large and she hoped the blush that was creeping up her neck was not noticeable. It was very hard to hide that this was the first man she'd kissed since Jake.

There was only one other guy in college that Gretchen had hooked up with when she and Jacob were taking a mutual break. Kent. He was a Sigma Chi with amazing fingers, played guitar and had seduced her at a party one night. It was one helluva night and she didn't realize her body could bend in those positions. But other than that one incident which didn't really count, she was no Hook-Up Queen. Gretchen wasn't made that way.

"Either. I don't usually take random women home. I am merely a man trying to make a living and very rarely have time for anything else. And, the other thing-you shouldn't ever lick your lips in front of a man wanting you the way I do." Grey thought to himself he was going to scare her off with his blatant statement. He was usually pretty good at keeping his wants and needs locked up tight. There must have been truth serum in her lipstick.

Gretchen grinned mischievously while she lifted his hand up to her face. She licked her well-kissed lips very slowly while looking up at him through her lashes. Then, she added a little moan and closed her eyes when she sucked one of his long, strong fingers into her hot, wet mouth. She knew what she wanted: one night with Grey.

Grey's throat went dry. He tried to swallow. His jeans were not as comfortable as they were when they left the club. "I warned you." With that said, he encircled her waist with both arms and pulled her to him, slightly raising her off her feet. His mouth began a gentle, sensual assault on hers and then moved down to her neck. His wet kisses alternated between soft, moist and curious to deep, wet and almost rough and it sent Gretchen into a new world. Grey's knee found a comfortable spot between her legs and she couldn't help but lean into the firm muscle under the denim. His sly hands found their way under her shirt to touch her back, his thumbs caressing her sides and stomach. His stroking fingers evoked desire until she could feel the moisture between her legs along with a pleasurable ache. Grey's hands moved to cup her breasts. When he found that they were larger than a handful, he groaned. His mouth watered to taste them.

He broke from the kiss long enough to pull them both under the cover of the tree. The streetlights, although fairly dim by the river, still made him feel like he was in the spotlight on a stage with their bright orbs. What he wanted to do was meant to be private.

"You have no idea what you do to me, Gretchen." Kissing her body was an appetizer to the main course. He sat on the bench under the tree and guided her to stand between his legs. His mouth lined up perfectly with her breasts. He lifted the shirt, bent his head to lay kisses on her stomach. She had a navel piercing and it was a skull and cross-bones.

A part of his anatomy jerked to full attention. Oh man. This was unexpected and immediately he wanted to be deep inside her. He stopped to lave her belly button and flicked the ring with his pointed tongue. Everything in Gretchen tightened and the sensation was extremely erotic. She ran her fingers through his hair and her feminine noises communicated she liked what he was doing. Grey said, "Oh babe, I'm just getting started. I want you to remember this night."

He moved his mouth over to her breasts and kissed the skin above her bra. It was all nude lace and he could see her tips begging for attention. Grey trailed wet kisses all the way to her nipples. He kissed and nipped them through the lace with one hand on the small of her back pressing her into his mouth. He moved to the other breast and did the same thing, pausing only to enjoy the pleasure on her flushed face. Grey thought to himself, I did that; he grinned and went back to loving her body in the heavy, New Orleans air.

His hand moved on her thigh under the denim. He reveled in the feeling of nothing but smooth Gretchen under the denim. Grey realized she must have been wearing a thong; his hands had made his way up to her waist under the skirt and had not encountered any fabric barriers. As he slid his hands around to grip her sweet behind, he swore and stood up.

"It's time to go." Grey bit out. He grabbed her hand. "Wh-what's wrong?" Gretchen was poleaxed. She thought things were progressing quite nicely. It was like trying to wake quickly from a drugged sleep.

"I can't wait any longer and of course, this is not a decent place to make love to you." His voice was strained and thick.

Grey began walking quickly and dragging her behind him. Trying to keep up, she stumbled and lost a flip-flop. "Hey, wait a minute. How are we getting back? The cabs are all around Jackson Square. I think it would be hard to walk in your condition let alone run." While she trapped her flip-flop with her big toe and pushed her foot into it, Grey pulled out his Blackberry and punched around on it.

In about three minutes, there were two silver H3 trucks on the street in front of them. A very dark skinned man that he addressed as Blake got out of the Hummer in the back, tossed him a set of keys and got in the other vehicle and rode off.

Grey walked over and opened the passenger door for Gretchen, then walked around to get in on the driver's side. Grey leaned over and kissed her and started the Hummer. "Do you want to know where we are going?"

Gretchen was more comfortable with Grey by the minute but she didn't even know his last name. "Yes, I do, but first I have a question."

"What is your last name?" She didn't know why she thought he would tell her, since he was a stranger in a bar that she just picked up. Or, did he pick up her?

"It's Maddock. Why do you ask?" Grey peered at her curiously.

"Grey Maddock." Gretchen rolled it off her tongue and Grey nearly melted in his seat. "Just wanted to know who I was going to spend some time with tonight and who my friends could look for if I don't come home." Gretchen smiled and looked at him coyly.

"Fair enough." Grey Maddock seemed to appreciate her honesty and nodded his head.

Grey said, "We are going to The Blue Note Hotel," to honor his statement of letting her know where he was taking her. As he took off from the curb in anxious anticipation of the next few hours, Gretchen sent Lou a text message to let her know the specifics of her plans for the evening.

As soon as she closed her phone, it rang and the display showed Jeb's face. Immediately, she opened the phone and said, "Hey honey, what's going on?"

Jeb voice came through, "Mom, I miss you and I don't want to be here. Daddy's got a date tonight and I just want to be at home in my own bed."

Gretchen's voice caught. She thought to herself, I don't know why that information should be surprising. She had known that Jake would need someone at home to do his laundry, cook his meals, write out the bills and warm his bed from time to time. Some women would have been happy to have only access to his checkbook, getting nothing else from him.

"Jeb, it's okay that he has a date. Where are you staying? Did he get Paige to come and stay with you?" Gretchen began to worry that he would leave Jeb at home alone. She was always uncomfortable alone in the farmhouse in the middle of BFE. Gretchen had learned to use a gun for that reason.

"Yes, Mom, but it's not like you and home." Jeb sounded forlorn and lonely.

"Aw, honey. It's going to be fun playing with Paige. Is she going to bring her puppy?" Gretchen's success with taking Jeb down a notch on the anxiety scale had been found with redirection.

"Well, yeah, Mom. She is and I guess that will be fun." Jeb's voice cheered and Gretchen was relieved. There was precious little she could do eight hours away to comfort her son.

"Atta boy. You have a great time with Paige and I'll see you in a few days. I'll bring you something neat back from New Orleans, kay?" Gretchen was hoping this was working to take care of her only child.

"Alright, Mom. Hey, Paige is here. Gotta run. Love you!" Before Gretchen had a moment to respond, he had disconnected. She smiled to herself and dropped the cell in her purse.

"Everything okay?" Grey was stopped at a light and turned in his seat to study her face.

"Oh, yeah. My son, Jeb." Gretchen waved the question away but her mind remained on him a moment longer.

"How old is he?" Grey was curious about Gretchen's child. He didn't have any of his own and didn't plan on having any, either. Again, he was too busy for those kinds of responsibilities.

"He is 10 years old going on 20. Jeb is a real joy in my life and also a real challenge, but I wouldn't change it for anything in the world." Gretchen beamed when she spoke of her son. Grey knew the look and had seen it on his mother's face. He gave her a sheepish grin and remembered that she wouldn't change it for anything in the world. The hummer made its way through the damp night air of New Orleans to the Blue Note Hotel. As they pulled in under the covered entrance for valet parking, Harry Connick, Jr. was belting out a sexy tune on the radio and the evening was just beginning.

Chapter Three

Quietly, Gretchen inserted the key card in the door slot. It was 7:30 a.m. and she and her friends were on vacation. She was trying to be quiet so as not to wake them. Sleep for grown women with full time jobs was a coveted commodity. Chances were that Lou had stayed with Sam. Cherie slept like the dead. It was almost an impossibility to disturb either of them. When she opened the door, things were not as she suspected.

Cherie and Lou screamed when they saw Gretchen come in the door. Based on the sight of her two friends, neither had slept much all night. "Oh. My. Gosh. We thought you had been chopped up in little pieces and thrown into the Mississippi or had been fed to the alligators in the swamps! We are so glad to see you!" Cherie had a thing for the dramatic. Gretchen immediately felt bad about not getting in touch with her friends periodically throughout the evening. Her cell phone battery had died at some point. She knew she was more than fine. And, she had sent a text to Lou.

Gretchen felt bad for making them worry and hugged both of their necks assuring them that she was safe from bodily injury most of the time. "I left a message with the front desk for you all. The message explained where I was and the man's full name. My cell died." She looked and the phone wouldn't even turn on. Digging around in her suitcase, she located the charger and plugged in her phone.

Lou was on the phone with Sam. Gretchen couldn't remember her ever looking so pissed off and so relieved all at the same time. "She just walked in the door. Can I report a crime before it happens because I'm getting ready to kill her." Lou paused to hear what Sam was saying on the other end. Her angry expression melted and she began blushing. "Yeah, I'm hungry, too. Call me when you get here." Lou's mood was much better after her phone conversation with Sam. On the way to the shower, she mentioned something about Sam coming to get her for brunch and being on his menu.

Cherie and Gretchen flopped down on the bed. Gretchen sighed. Cherie yawned and said, "Must have been one heck of a night for you to come in at 7:30 in the morning and sigh like that."

"Yeah, it was pretty great. There's nothing like spending the night with a total stranger. That was so unlike me. He was different, though, Cherie. He was kind of normal. I guess I expected a womanizing pervert with no class. I got the feeling that he didn't pick up women all the time." She smiled and shrugged.

Cherie began braiding Gretchen's hair. "So, tell me about it. Was the night your biggest fantasy in the flesh? Did he have a big, thick, capable . . ."

"Cherie!" Gretchen rolled her eyes to Cherie's point blank questioning. Cherie was in stitches at Gretchen's response. She would freak if she only knew the answer to her last question. "His name is Grey Maddock. He has a ship company based out of the Caribbean. St. Barts island I think he said. Remember when I went diving off of St. Bart's on that sunken ship? His company, family owned and operated, sank it for recreational diving. He works with his mother, Clare and a few employees. His father is no longer living."

Gretchen smiled remembering the last twelve hours. She also realized that was the reason behind the warm face at the bar. He was literally at home. Mental head smack. Why did she second-guess everything? "He was a real gentleman. I don't think I will forget him."

"Girl, I knew this is just what you needed! So, is he going to call you? Did you leave him your digits? It wouldn't hurt to keep in touch in case you are both in the area again." Cherie sounded hopeful.

"I gave him my email address. I thought that was enough. Cherie, I don't think I will hear from him let alone ever see him again. I had fun for a night and he was a nice guy that definitely knew what he was doing." Gretchen grinned. "Besides, the three of us came to New Orleans for Mardi Gras and to spend time together. Let's go get some coffee and beignets at the Café DuMonde. I'm feeling like fighting a large pigeon for a powdered sugared pastry."

Gretchen left Lou a note to let her know where they were going and to call when she was back at the room. The friends planned to do a little sightseeing during the day. It might take awhile for Lou to return from brunch with Sam. He was an attorney and he didn't quit until his point was made with the jury. The same went with Lou. She needed lots of convincing and Sam was The Man for the job.

On the way to the Café, Gretchen used Cherie's phone to call her son. Jeb answered on the third ring. "Hello?"

"Jeb, honey, it's your Mom. How are you doing?"

"Oh, hey Mom. Why aren't you calling on your cell?" Jeb was a smart boy and the caller ID was connected through the satellite. The number Jeb didn't recognize showed up on the flat screen. He loved telling his mom who was calling. That was when it was their TV. Now it was just Jake and Jeb's.

"Well, my battery is dead and it's charging in the room. What have you and your Dad been doing?"

"Oh Mom, we've spent a lot of time at the store. I made ten dollars by helping Poppa Bill unload the last shipment of filters. There was a skunk in the truck and it almost sprayed us! We ran fast. I've never seen Poppa run like that." His excited voice made Gretchen have mixed emotions. She missed him terribly, but she needed a break from her real world.

"A skunk? Boy, that was a close one and you could be stinking until your next birthday. What else are you up to?"
"Um, not much Mom. I'll let you talk to my Dad now." He wasn't much of a telephone talker and he handed the phone to Jake.

"Hi Gretchen." Jacob's deep, country boy voice came clearly across the line. Her gut gave a tight squeeze. Jake's voice would probably elicit that response for the rest of her life. She was sad their marriage didn't work out.

"Hello Jacob. Jeb sounds like he is having a good time. I'm really glad."

"Yep." Jake was not a big talker on the telephone or in person. Gretchen just wished he would find someone to make him blissfully happy. She thought that probably wasn't a person, but more like a thing-his own chain of hardware stores. Jacob wanted to have his own place and do things the way he wanted to. He was not a man that likes to follow directions, even from his father. He had his own ideas. Having a chain of stores was very expensive. Gretchen had always referred to the hardware store as his expensive hobby because it took time and money away from the family and didn't give much back. Gretchen resented the hell out of it.

"Well, I called on Cherie's cell phone because mine is charging. Call on this number if Jeb needs anything. Please tell him bye for me and that I love him." She disconnected and passed the cell back to Cherie.

By then, Cherie had found them a table and they had their breakfast in front of them. Gretchen took a deep breath. "OK, hit me." Cherie handed her a beignet. She held it close to her nose and inhaled. "How in the world do they get all this yummy goodness in this little pillow puff of dough with powdered sugar on it?" She took a sip of her coffee. Now that was good.

Cherie, who had a very high metabolism, dove into her beignet and could probably eat a dozen before they started to show on her figure. Gretchen, on the other hand, gained weight just by smelling one. But the coffee was Cherie's favorite. "Without my coffee, I don't think I would be human! That's why I could never have lived in caveman times. Well, that and no pedicurists."

Gretchen giggled with her mouth full of bliss and nodded. She covered her mouth with her napkin. The powdered sugar was blowing around in the breeze. Large gray pigeons stood guard by many tables in hopes of a forgotten beignet. When anything dropped on the patio, the pigeons flogged it.

The day was pleasant and she enjoyed being outside with her beignet and coffee. Cherie's company was always entertaining. She was also a good friend. They shared opinions on many things and it was an easy friendship.

Cherie had her own photography studio and was married to a man whom she met in college. Her husband, Jeff Strenson, was the town veterinarian and was well liked. They had a full life complete with nine dogs. Those were their babies.

Cherie had a spirit of independence and strength. She, Lou, and Gretchen had that in common. That was one of the things that drew these ladies together. They also shared the joy of diving into a good romance or mystery novel. Here she was, once again, being a friend to Gretchen by taking off work to be with her.

Gretchen reached out and touched Cherie's arm. She looked her in the face and said, "Cherie, thank you so much for taking off to come down here with me. You will never know how much your support and friendship has meant to me. I think without you and Lou, I would have not made it this far. You have been so many things to me and for me. I love ya, girl."

Cherie rolled her eyes. She smiled with a wink and said, "Oh good grief! Don't start ruining a perfectly good beignet with tears and snot." Cherie knew she was sincere, but she didn't want it to turn into a full-on crying session.

Gretchen laughed out loud. Cherie always knew how to lighten the mood. "You are right. I can't have that happen. Let's run over to the Market and see what they have. They have the best stuff there!" They finished their beignets and coffee and headed off for the French Market. Gretchen loved to shop there because of the unique items for sale and you never knew what you could find there.

Brussels sprouts. Red bell peppers. Apples. Oranges. Grey Maddock. Corn. Okra. What? Did she really see Grey standing there looking at the produce? She would recognize his shoulders anywhere. The memory of Grey's broad shoulders hovering over her as he made love to her would be unforgettable.

She couldn't believe he was here in the market. He was wearing a pair of khaki cargo shorts and hemp flip-flops with a red homemade muscle shirt. The man was fine in whatever he put on his body. He was also fine in nothing. She knew that firsthand.

Gretchen made her way around the green beans so that she was standing in front of him with the vegetable stand between them. He had reading glasses perched on his straight nose and was studying a peach with intensity. She'd never seen anything so sexy in all her life than Grey with reading glasses. It made him human. She thought of the night before and she wished to be the peach in his hand.

Grey stood in front of the produce. He picked up a peach and examined it and thought of his night with Gretchen. Now why would looking at a peach make him think of her? He felt how soft the skin was, like Gretchen. He thought about the juice inside and about how sweet it tastes and well, hell, that was Gretchen, too. The way she looked as he made love to her was a memory he was reliving right here in the French Market. He could almost smell her. That couldn't be possible, could it? He looked up over his glasses and thought he was imagining her.

"Gretchen?" Grey couldn't believe his eyes.

Gretchen sent him a coy smile and gave a nod. "Grey."

Grey looked back at the peach and then put it down. Not knowing what to do, he just looked at her and said with a shrug, "I was just shopping for some produce. The Market has the best stuff." He should have said he was also thinking of her, but didn't want to frighten her off.

Cherie was beside her and she said quietly for Gretchen's ears only, "Mmm hmm. It sho' does have the best stuff. Where can I get me some of that?" Cherie was saying it as she flicked her wrist and pointed at the man in the red muscle shirt.

It was for Gretchen's comic relief since she was happily married. Cherie knew they needed a few minutes alone and said, "I'm going to look over here at these books. Maybe I can learn something about the Cajun peeps before we head north." Cherie moved on down the aisle. Gretchen stared after her for a moment, smiling and shaking her head.

She turned her head back to Grey and said, "Cherie and I just had coffee and beignets and are killing a little time until Lou gets back." Gretchen felt the awkwardness sneaking in. She didn't know what to do with her hands or where her eyes should rest. What do you say to a man you don't really know when you've spent several hours making love with him? Especially with several bushels of green beans separating you. She finally decided to be interested in the cucumbers in front of her.

"Oh, yeah?" He was sure Gretchen thought he was blowing her off. But, Grey just wanted to feed her the peach and then kiss her sweet, peachy lips.

He couldn't make any other words form in his mouth. Why was he having this reaction? Admittedly, she made him come harder than any other woman. He actually saw stars. No, that was not true. He rode the Milky Way. 'Oh yeah' is the most intelligent thing a man with a Ph.D. in Marine Biology could mumble to a woman who rocked his world not even eight hours ago? If he didn't think of something better to say, she would be gone.

Gretchen was so embarrassed. She didn't think he was interested in her, as a person, just as a good time. Well what did she expect? She had to figure out how to unglue her feet from the floor and start moving away from this nightmare. The pain of his rejection was making it hard to breathe.

Once she found her voice she told Grey, "Well, enjoy your fruit." Her feet finally decided to cooperate and she started walking towards Cherie. Why did she allow last night to happen? It was very un-Gretchen like, but she did it anyway. This kind of new and exciting life was not all it was cracked up to be.

Grey stood there by the beans and mumbled to himself, "Good one, Maddock." He watched her meet up with her friend and then hastily exit the Market. She was gone.

As she walked toward Cherie the tears were threatening to spill over. "Hey, what do you think of this book? I might find some use for this . . . Gretchen, oh my gosh, what's the matter?" Cherie had turned to find her friend with little rivers running silently down her cheeks. Cherie knew it was time to leave the Market. "Was that Mr. One Nighter? What did he say to you? Do I need to go and inflict bodily harm on that man?" Cherie narrowed her eyes at her friend. Her temper was rising, but she was trying to infuse some humor into the situation to cheer Gretchen.

"I was just dumb, I guess. I don't know anything anymore. I don't know what I expected from a man after a one-night stand." Gretchen was trying to get herself together and was failing miserably. She had to get out of the French Market before she started blubbering or had to honk her nose into a tissue. She definitely did not want Grey to see or hear that. She expected the emotional tide to come in, but why here in the French Market in New Orleans? Why couldn't it be while she was sitting in the bathtub drinking a bottle of wine? They quickly exited the Market and sat on a bench.

Cherie's phone rang in her purse. It was Lou and she was back in the room. Cherie briefly relayed to Lou about Gretchen bumping into the man from the bar in the French Market. Lou groaned. "Are ya'll coming back to the hotel now?"

"Yes, we are on our way in a bit." Cherie glanced over at Gretchen. She nodded at Cherie that she was ready to journey back. Gretchen just wanted some pain reliever and a bed. Not that she could sleep with all the caffeine she had for breakfast. It would be hard enough to ignore the scenes that continued to play in her head from last night and of course the most recent, mortifying one in the Market. Maybe if she could sleep she would wake feeling much better. The ladies had plans to see the evening's parades.

They arrived back at the hotel and she climbed into bed after taking some pain reliever and downing a large glass of water. Surprisingly, Gretchen felt herself doze off. The bed was so comfortable; the room was dark and quiet.

Gretchen's eyes were so scratchy as she tried to regain consciousness from her napping. She didn't think her body would allow her to get up even if the bed was on fire. It felt so good to snuggled further down into the feather bed. But her friends had traveled all this way just for her. She dug deep, found some motivation and rolled from the bed.

After Gretchen had showered, she felt better. It was easy to feed off of the energy Lou and Cherie put off. The ladies were pumped to be going to a Mardi Gras parade. They made their way downstairs and out onto the street. It was a sea of bodies undulating like the waves on the beach and the pulse of the crowd was palpable. Some of the bodies were dressed up and some of them barely were covered. Most all had beads and masks and were enjoying the weeklong celebration.

Gretchen and her friends caught beads and noisemakers thrown off the floats. Subconsciously, she scanned the crowd for a familiar body. Grey mentioned he might be coming to Bourbon Street that night. If he was there, she didn't see him. With all the people he would be easy to miss.

As the parade ended, the girls made their way back to the hotel to shower off the funk of the experience. Gretchen enjoyed the evening with her girlfriends, but she didn't know if she wanted to be at Mardi Gras again. For her, it might be one of those things where you said you've done it once.

She could definitely say that it was interesting. There was a woman who stripped for the crowd while standing on a trashcan. The girls witnessed many people urinating in the streets-male and female. Regrettably, they witnessed what happened when your body had too many tequila oyster shooters. Gretchen thought the word 'lewd' was created after being on Bourbon Street during Mardi Gras. Several couples would definitely qualify for a picture beside the word in the dictionary. And, she didn't see Grey.

The next five nights were the same party with different drinks. Each night Gretchen hoped to see Grey. He knew where she was staying, but he didn't try to contact her. By now, if he were going to call, he would have. Grey was a 'one-nighter' kind of guy after all.

The girls hit the margaritas hard on Fat Tuesday. Everyone was trying to get the last of the partying in before Ash Wednesday, which marked the beginning of Lent. The floats were bigger and more outrageous. The crowd was bigger and more outrageous. The night drew to a close for the women and it was time to go back to the room for some much needed sleep.

The three friends got on the elevator. Lou had an especially unusual set of beads around her neck. Cherie said, "Hey sis, where did you get those?"

"Hmphf. Wouldn't you like to know?" Lou smiled like the proverbial cat that ate the canary.

"Uh, no, I wouldn't. Gross, Lou!" Cherie eyes went wide. Then, Cherie shook her head and laughed. One way to get beads at Mardi Gras was to flash a private body part to the holder of the beads. If they liked what they saw, then you caught the beads they tossed. Gretchen was glad she wasn't standing beside her when she earned those.

"When in Rome..." Lou let her statement fade off while she grinned.

Gretchen just smiled and shook her head. "Well, this has been real all the way around. I've had a blast. Maybe now I'll have a fresh attitude for work if I can find the energy to return to work! I'll at least have some funny things to think about." The elevator dinged and they were on their floor.

She pushed herself off the rail of the elevator and shuffled to the room. The hotel was quieter than they expected. Of course it was 6 a.m. They had enough time to shower and sleep a few hours before a late check out at 1 p.m.

After showers and naps, the women packed up and checked out. The weather had turned cooler and the skies were gray and overcast. It was a good thing that Gretchen brought her jacket. Even with the jacket, she still had a chill; she thought it had nothing to do with the windy day or the 52-degree temperature. Leaving Louisiana was a downer. The real world was "imminent."

When it was her turn to drive, Cherie and Lou fell quickly asleep. She was left to her own thoughts and Gretchen began to think about returning to her job. She liked what she did and the pay was decent; she just needed to relocate.

Her career as a nurse consultant was flexible. She liked the freedom to work from her home and not have holiday, weekend or night shifts to cover. The corporate headquarters didn't have a preference where she made her office as long as the facilities could reach her when they had a question. They all had her cell phone number and were able to contact her. She did provide trainings for them, but it was only twice a year. She could drive the distance.

Gretchen loved the warmer climate and had often thought of moving south. She just couldn't get the logistics straight in her head of how she could make that happen with a child and a husband who owned his own business. Now maybe she would revisit those options.

She anticipated seeing her son, Jeb, and his bright face and intelligent eyes. Rolling her eyes, Gretchen also looked forward to putting Grey Maddock in her past, if she ever could. She wondered what happened with Grey. Gretchen thought he might call her while she was still in New Orleans.

Clare Maddock had telephoned Grey the morning he took Gretchen back to her hotel. "Grey, honey. I need you to come back to the office and sign some papers. The deal went through on transferring the project in New Orleans to Black Cove Shipping Co. You are off the hook."

"Oh, Mom, thank you! I was really beginning to loathe this project. I couldn't get anything done. I have plenty to do at home. You wouldn't have already booked my flight would you?" Part of Grey wanted to fly back to the island today and get going on his projects at home. The other part of him was thinking on the new project he had found in New Orleans: Gretchen Mitchell.

Grey was a sailor at heart. GMS, Incorporated was Greyson Maddock Shipping, Inc. It was the ship business his mom and dad had built from the ground up based only on their love of sailing. He and his mother, Clare Maddock, were the heads of the small, but successful company.

Grey had lost his dad in an accident twelve years ago that left him feeling very responsible for the circumstances of the event. Ever since that day, Grey had not really let himself live life to the fullest; why should he be happy when his father was not here? He guarded his feelings and his thoughts because he didn't want to be hurt like that again.

There had been women in Grey's life on a very casual basis. Mostly the women were looking for something more than the sailboat tour of the island. That really wasn't his thing. Not one of them inspired him to be open and honest with them.

He never took the few women in whose company he found himself to his cottage, only his guesthouse. The cottage seemed fitting for only someone who was worthy of it. He couldn't explain the feeling, but he thought he would know the right woman when she came into his life. His mother's voice jarred him from his reverie.

"Yes, Greyson, I did. You leave at 1420. so you better get your bags packed and yourself to the airport." His mother was always pleased to take care of her son. Clare knew he didn't need it, but she did it anyway.

"Alright then, Mom. Thanks." Grey sighed and hung up with his mom. Well, maybe the fates were talking and it was time to go back home. Maybe the fates were telling him to enjoy what he had and remember Gretchen, but move on. Maybe he should tell the fates to hush because he had her email address.

Chapter Four

Booting up her MacBook, Gretchen sighed. It was Thursday morning, her first day back from vacation and it was back to work. She had several messages to respond to from her facilities. Jeb was off to school and she could give the emails her undivided attention. Several emails were easy to answer.

As she scrolled down, a sender that she didn't recognize was on the list of new mail. It was from topbananagmm@gmm.com Gretchen clicked on the email to open it and just about fell out of her office chair. It was from Grey Maddock. Her lips moved as her eyes scanned the words he wrote:

Gretchen,

Hey, it's Grey. Just wanted to see if this email goes   through. I hope so. I will remember the time we spent together. You are an amazing woman. I'm sorry I was weird in the Market. I was taken by surprise to see you there. If you are ever considering returning to St.   Bart's, let me know. I have a proper and personal welcome waiting for you. Email me back and let me know you got this. I'll be in touch.

See you babe, Grey

Gretchen stared at the screen. She couldn't believe he had emailed her. She sure hadn't expected him to. Gretchen had almost forgotten about giving it to him. There were several more work-related issues on which to focus, so she closed his email without responding.

She addressed the questions and concerns, and clarified some of the rules of licensing, answered some nursing issues. Some she was able to answer by email. Many required a telephone call. There were two communities that she would have to visit and review charts and help to get new staff and do some training for a new employee. She didn't mind to get out of the house. The short drive might help her mind decide what to reply to Grey Maddock.

She gathered her coat and gloves. The Missouri air was a chilly thirty-seven degrees. It was quite a brutal change from the flip-flop and denim skirt weather in Louisiana. Her thoughts wandered further south to much warmer things as her car cruised down the highway.

The warm salty breeze of the Caribbean, the beautiful water, the green eyes of Grey Maddock were all thoughts that kicked up her internal thermometer and soon she didn't need her coat and gloves. She shouldn't be entertaining any ideas about the Caribbean or Mr. Green Eyes. Just because the sex was so great she'd lost a brain cell or two didn't mean that it would be any more than sex. But, a woman could dream, couldn't she? And, he *had* emailed her.

She arrived at the facility and didn't have a decision about what to say to Grey. As Gretchen entered the facility, Gretchen remembered why she consulted for the skilled nursing facilities. It was her desire to help people.

She had a soft heart and she did what was necessary to help others even to the point of sacrificing herself. She had worked as a charge nurse in long term care facilities and even had been a director of nursing in a Residential Care Facility for a short time. With a small child at home, it was very hard trying to cover the shifts and be a good mom and wife.

Jacob worked incessantly and she was on-call for the facility every other week. That meant Jeb stayed with his Poppa Bill a lot. She rarely saw her family.

Gretchen happened to be in the corporate office when the nurse consultant job became available. She saw it as an opportunity to have a career and a family. After five years, she was still consulting.

Gretchen spent the majority of her late morning in the facility with the director of nursing, who was a new employee and had several questions for her. When her consulting was done for the day, she made her way back to town to pick up Jeb from school; some days, she never had to leave her house.

Gretchen's cell phone rang and it was Lou. "Hello, this is Lou. You have plans for supper tonight?"

Gretchen said, "No, not really. What's up?"

"Margaritas are on my menu. How about a Thirsty Thursday?" Lou and Gretchen would get together from time to time to drink their supper and had clever names and excuses for their binges. Jake was gone often when they were married and took Jeb with him to the store. Gretchen was left to her own devices and one of them just happened to be tequila.

"Sounds good to me. Come on out. I have an email I would like for you to read." Gretchen closed her phone as she pulled into the school parking lot. Jeb was waiting for his mother and he was impatient. His attitude improved when he realized his dad was coming to get him to go to the hardware store after school.

There was always something to entertain Jeb at the store. He was excited and hoped that he would get a chance to show Poppa Bill how he learned to count coins today at school. Gretchen just smiled and shook her head. The boy shared the love of money with his dad.

Chapter Five

"Well, have you emailed him back?" Lou asked after reading Grey's email. She sat back in the office chair, removed her reading glasses and took a long sip from her margarita, stopping to lick some of the salt off the rim. She looked up at Gretchen waiting for her reply.

"Nope. What do you say to a man you know intimately but don't know personally?" Gretchen wanted to do more than just email him. Since being with Grey, her hormones had been in overdrive. Maybe that was the Margarita talking. Jose Cuervo had been known to do some thinking and even acting for her from time to time.

"You know what I think?" Gretchen knew Lou was getting ready to tell her like it was. She loved her honesty most of the time. "I think you should email him back something fairly benign. I also think you should book a plane ticket to St. Barts, French West Indies. He practically told you that he would be your personal tour guide. Don't you have some ideas what he means by that? Cherie said he was one hot man. And, he did apologize for the weirdness in the French `Market`. He didn't even have to email you. I think you should go for it."

Lou was a fly-by-the-seat-of-her-pants kind of woman with a zest for every day of her life. Get It Together was her dream: organizing other people's stuff. She was very successful. Owning her own business from home allowed her to have the funds and the time to travel around the world to chase whatever she chose. Gretchen didn't quite have it together like Lou.

"I knew you would say that. I guess I just needed to hear it. I think I will start with emailing him back. I might wait a day or two before booking the plane ticket." She smiled and winked at Lou. Gretchen turned to go back to the kitchen for another drink. She would need more liquid courage and the margaritas were especially good tonight.

After Lou left for the evening and Jeb had taken his shower and was in bed, Gretchen sat down to reply to Grey's message. After several attempts at what to say, she decided on:

Grey,

It was good to hear from you. I enjoyed myself, too. I didn't know what to think of how you reacted in the Market.   It was weird for me, too. I've never had a night with a   man like that before and honestly didn't know what to   expect afterwards. Good luck with your next project.   If I'm ever in the Caribbean again, I'll definitely look you up. Email when you can.

Until later, Gretchen

It could be fun to have an email buddy. It would be hard for her to date anyone with ten-year-old Jeb. She just didn't want to expose him to different men. Now, if she found one that was a keeper, she might feel differently. Right now she was doing well to find a new 'normal' for her and Jeb and that was her top priority. Finding a new life was something that would just take time. She seemed to have plenty of it these days.

Before long, winter turned to spring. Jeb began doing more outside projects with scouts. The ladies met once a month for dinner and drinks. Gretchen shared her latest Grey emails.   Summer passed in a frenzied blur. It was the busiest of summers that she could remember. Jeb was either gone with his dad to the store, was in the pool in the backyard or was getting ready for the fall cub scout retreat.

Her facilities had trainings and in-services for her to complete for the year as well. Gretchen was teaching nurses how to use the new intravenous pumps, glucometers and pulse oximeters. She taught so many classes of CPR she thought her lips would fall off.

At times her lips felt like they did after Grey Maddock was through kissing them: spent and plump. She missed kissing him. She longed for his scent on her skin and her sheets. She would love to be in the Caribbean with him, but she only had time to think about it.

Finally, things settled some when Jeb started back to school. It was busy, but a different kind. She was back to working mostly from home at her computer or on the phone. Gretchen had successfully created a new normal for her and Jeb and it felt pretty good.

Chapter Six

Taking a break from consulting, Gretchen stood at the back door watching the fall leaves blowing around in the backyard. She took a sip of her hot tea. Fall was her favorite time of year with the crisp cool air and the trees with their vibrant colors.

She couldn't believe how much time had passed since her divorce. Jeb and her had developed a good routine at home and he was adjusting well. He still spent time with his Dad at the hardware store almost every day after school. He would spend some weekends with Gretchen and some with his Dad. As far as Jeb was concerned, Jake and Gretchen were getting along fine. They didn't really fight they just didn't talk about anything else.

Her computer alerted her that she had an email. She had been sporadically corresponding with Grey Maddock since February. The last six weeks the intensity had ratcheted up a level or two. Now, they communicated at least daily sometimes more often and had even started talking on the telephone. Something that started out as being quasi-casual email buddies that had slept together had developed into a strong friendship. It could have been more had they lived closer to each other.

On occasion, Grey would call her on the weekends that Jeb was gone to his Dad's to visit. It was always nice to hear his voice. Sometimes they would use the webcam and be able to see each other. He would explain how the customers that booked the sailing tours were rewarding or sometimes frustrating, but always entertaining. She would share what was going on in the world of nursing consultation and later, Jeb. His timing was perfect for making jokes and saying the kind word when Gretchen's day was rough.

It was like he and Gretchen had known each other for longer than five months. Grey shared a lot about himself. It was strange how close they had gotten over a couple of keyboards and computer screens.

She learned that his parents, Greyson and Clare Maddock, started his company, Greyson Maddock Shipping, Incorporated. The couple had visited the Caribbean on their honeymoon. While there, the newly weds fell in love with sailing and decided to make St. Barts their home. Within a year they had their company up and running with two small sailboats. Since that time, the company had bought several sailboats that they rented commercially complete with a skipper and first mate. Now, this was the bulk of their business. They had also sunk ten ships all over the world for various reasons.

Grey was born knowing how to tie a bowline knot and how to tell the difference between a sloop and a schooner. He often went to work with his father who affectionately called him his Top Banana. Hence, the email address was an appropriate choice for him. Grey's father was his mentor and best friend. What he learned from his Dad was more valuable than anything he learned in the classroom.

Right out of high school, his mother, Clare, insisted he go to college even though he planned to work with his Dad and eventually take over the family business. So, he had reluctantly gone to college in Miami and earned a degree in Marine Biology.

He returned to St. Barts island to work with his father until he lost him in an accident a little over twelve years ago. He was still very upset about it and didn't elaborate about what really happened. Gretchen almost asked him about it, but decided it might not be the time or place. He went on to share that it was later in his thirties that he took online classes to get his doctorate. About twice a year, he spoke at Florida State to the undergraduates about the fragile ecosystem of the Caribbean.

Grey had been married once when he was very young to a girl named Kate. He called her a girl since she was only 19 and he 23 when they wed. He lightly joked that he didn't have any children that he was acquainted with, but he wouldn't mind having one around. He said he might even enjoy it.

After 42 years on this earth, he decided he loved the taste of grilled asparagus, green beans, shrimp, lasagna and cheeseburgers. He had typed, "really I like just about anything that doesn't eat me first." And of course, Crown Royal and Coke was his drink of choice when sweet tea wasn't available.

Grey loved to spear fish for sport, which intrigued Gretchen. She would have to check that out when and if she ever made it down to St. Barts. His middle name was Michael and he had a great amount of love and respect for the woman he called Mom. He was allergic to red dye and cinnamon. Grey had the chicken pox at age seven and often went commando. The latter part she already knew from their night in The Big Easy. He appeared to be an honest and successful man and he cooked. The friendship was more than comfortable. What else did she need to know?

Gretchen had shared with Grey about her country upbringing and the importance of her grandparents in her life. She too shared her middle name, Rae, and her maiden name Westin. She kept Jacob's last name of Mitchell since she had Jeb. She told the story of how she and Jacob met in high school and married.

Her life with Jake was mainly work and there was little playtime. Jake was a good man, but he didn't know how to relax and have fun. Her sister always said Jacob was like vanilla ice cream while she was more like a Sundae. Grey chuckled when she explained her sister's opinion.

Gretchen explained a little to Grey about why she divorced a man that provided financially for she and Jeb and was faithful to his marriage vows. Gretchen had told Grey about her memories of her ninth wedding anniversary. Jake asked Gretchen, "What do you want for our anniversary?"

Gretchen liked jewelry and said, "A diamond tennis bracelet." She asked more for the response from Jake than for the actual item.

For their anniversary Gretchen picked a nice restaurant, made the reservation and they went out for dinner. While they were eating Jake said to her, "Since you've managed your money so well, we'll go get you that tennis bracelet." Gretchen didn't know what to say.

They went to the jewelry store. Jake hardly even looked at what Gretchen was picking out. He stood around looking out the store window and wanted to know the cost. Then, when Gretchen picked out the one she wanted, she wrote the check for it.

Gretchen felt so unloved and disposable, like Jake could get another one just like her. The next time around, he would get one who couldn't care less if he was involved in their relationship. She was sure the next wife would be happy to just have access to his checkbook and to show off whatever she could buy with his money.

She was done with her emotional part of the marriage on that day, but stayed in the marriage trying to make it work. Gretchen didn't enter into the marriage casually and they had a child. Those two things held her to being Mrs. Jacob Mitchell for three more years before she could no longer sacrifice herself. Greyson didn't blame her for feeling hurt.

When she revealed to Grey that she had a son, he was only mildly surprised. In the Midwest nearly everyone married and had children. That's just what the majority of people did. Once her secret was out and Grey didn't turn tail and run, Gretchen couldn't say enough about Jeb.

He was the apple of her eye and the biggest reason she got out of bed every morning. Grey didn't have to guess that she loved her son very much. She was a den mother for a group of ten-year-old boys. Greyson knew that took lots of love and patience and spoke highly of Gretchen's strength and perseverance.

Their conversations were intimate at times. She wanted to reach through the computer screen and touch his face and kiss his lips. Many times, when he reminded her of their evening spent together and the intensity of the conversation spiked to sensual level, she would later touch herself in her bed and fantasize about his clever fingers working on her.

She wished he lived closer so that they could at least drive to see each other. She missed his masculine smell that was a mixture of soap and Grey. He had even mailed her the blue t-shirt he was wearing the night they met. She had slept in it every night the last month, wishing it was him touching her instead of just a piece of his clothing. Gretchen was slowly going insane wanting him in her bed.

Chapter Seven

She only had hours to wait. Grey was finally coming to Missouri! He had agreed to come to St. Louis to talk with corporate executives at a brewery about an upcoming retreat for their employees in the Caribbean.

He often coordinated with the local hotels to promote his commercial sailing expeditions. They in turn would arrange meetings with potential customers to promote their hospitality and amenities. Customers would have great accommodations and experiences while on St. Barts. Grey would be a great host.

Grey had been more than willing to fly up thinking he might get to see Gretchen if he played his cards right. He had made plans for a rental car. After the meeting, he hopped in the car to drive down to Gretchen's.

This was a woman he wanted in his life more than just over the phone or on the computer. He wanted to be able to kiss her anytime he felt like it. Grey Maddock ached to feel Gretchen Mitchell move beneath him. He had shared so much of himself and he was unsure of exactly when he decided to take the leap of faith to open up. It wasn't a conscious decision, or at least he thought it wasn't.

When he would email her, he would often be in the guesthouse. But, lately when he would call her, he would be at the cottage. Sometimes he would put the phone on speaker to cook and talk to her. It wasn't long before he carried the phone all over the house on speaker to hear her voice in his living room and eventually in his master suite.

Gretchen Rae Mitchell could be The One for whom the cottage was built. Grey sat down on his couch and looked out at the ocean gently lapping at the beach. This thought was an elephant to eat, let alone digest.

When his mother had said that a brewery in St. Louis, Missouri was interested in bringing a group down, he volunteered to come to them. Clare didn't understand why he would volunteer and said, "Well, I hope this is about a woman." Grey turned an incredulous look on his mother, then hugged and kissed her goodbye.

The flight was uneventful, but his insides were churning. He was glad he didn't check any baggage because he couldn't wait to get to the car rental desk and be on the road to see his Missouri woman.

He had been connected to Gretchen on the cell phone from the time he left the airport rental desk until he pulled into her drive. He made great time and arrived sooner than he thought he would. "Now, tell me what color your house is again? I don't want to miss it."

"It's the color of yellow cake mix. It has dark green shutters on it and a big front porch with a white railing. You can't miss it. It's in the middle of a grove of pecan trees. What time are you going to be here?" She was trying to make cookies and finish her work before Grey arrived. Her level of anticipation was through the roof. She had taken a few days off work to be with him or to recuperate from being with him, whatever the case may be. She was hoping for the latter.

"Babe, look out your window." She went to the front of the house and saw him. Grey was standing on her front porch. He looked just as good as the first time she saw him in the bar. Grey was wearing faded denim jeans and a long sleeved heather green t-shirt and tennis shoes. His hair had grown longer but his skin was still just as brown as a biscuit.

She burst through the door and jumped into his arms. He supported her weight as she wrapped her legs around his waist. Grey laughed and turned a circle with her in his arms. The phone lay on the porch where it dropped from her hands, forgotten. She rained kisses on his face and on his neck, pausing only to breathe him in. She loved his smell of all warm man. He returned the kisses and squeezed her bottom with both hands. "Gretchen, you smell so good. You smell like something to eat."

"Promise?" She said teasingly as she leaned back to look into his eyes.

"Yes, but I mean you really smell like real food." Grey was glad he was here in Missouri with Gretchen. He couldn't stop the big grin that was permanent on his face.

"Oh, my gosh! I forgot about the cookies!" Gretchen jumped down from his arms and rushed into the house. Grey bent to pick up the abandoned phone and followed her into the house.

The peanut butter cookies were past the point of edible. Even on the cookie stone that advertised that nothing would burn, they were hopeless pieces of charcoal. She was trying to be a little domestic for Grey for reasons she couldn't quite admit to herself. "I'm sorry about the cookies. Can I get you something to drink instead of a cookie? I picked up some Crown and Coke." She began pouring herself a glass of wine. He nodded and she retrieved a highball glass from the cabinet. She got him some ice and he mixed his own drink.

Gretchen looked so good to him, better than any peanut butter cookie by a long shot. She had decided to put a few highlights in her long curly auburn hair and it lay on her olive green shirt, which was open to the third pearly button. She had retained most of her summer tan by laying in the tanning bed that she treated herself to with the company bonus. Her jeans fit perfectly over her curves, especially since she had kept up her exercise regime. She had on a little eyeliner and some shiny lip-gloss. Most of the lip-gloss didn't make it past the assault on the front porch.

"I didn't come all this way to have peanut butter cookies, babe. You look so good to me." Grey held her gaze. "Where's Jeb?" Grey was ready to meet Jeb. He was also anxious to get inside Gretchen, but he was trying to be polite and keep things cool, for now. He looked around the open design house from the kitchen.

Gretchen couldn't believe that Grey was standing in her kitchen. A touchable, kissable Grey was here, in her house and she had him all to herself. "Jeb is gone on a weekend camping retreat with the Cub Scout pack. I didn't have my outdoor training completed, so one of the other ladies volunteered to take my place. Maybe you can meet him the next time." Gretchen stood at the sink trying to get the burnt offering off the cookie sheet.

"What? Jeb isn't even home and you are still dressed and in the kitchen? Why are we wasting time in here, woman?" Grey smiled sexily and pulled her against him. She could feel his body heat and muscles. She turned and rubbed her hands over his chest and couldn't wait to remove his shirt and be skin on skin.

He began to nibble on her mouth, chin and neck. He got around to her ear and remembered his gift. "Oh, I have something for you."

"Well, I wondered how long you were going to make me wait for it." It was Gretchen's turn for the sexy smile. She waggled her eyebrows.

Grey wagged his finger in front of her face and laughed. "No, babe. Not that, although I'm quite impatient to make love to you." Grey trailed a finger down her cheek and stared at her mouth. "It's something else." He ran out to the rental car and she stood at the door.

While she watched him retrieve an overnight bag and a small package, she enjoyed the way his jeans caressed his firm backside. His t-shirt pulled tight across his wide shoulders as he reached into the car. She thought she heard a female whimper. Must have come from her.

Gretchen was thinking out loud. "I don't want anything but you in my bed all weekend long. I might let you up to shower and eat but then it's back to bed." All the emails and phone conversations they had weren't enough. She wanted Grey Maddock in the flesh and in her bed in a very wicked way.

She opened the screen door for him curious about the gift. Gretchen saw his excitement about it. The package was small and plainly wrapped. Grey frowned and said, "I was afraid to put a bow on it because it might get smashed in the carry-on compartment. Some of those people are not very nice and they carry larger bags than they are supposed to. Anyway, open it and then I will explain."

They sat down side-by-side on the couch and Gretchen began tearing the paper away. It was a small rectangular box and when she opened it, she gasped. It was a coral necklace and earrings. It appeared to be hand crafted. Grey said, "I went diving in the Cayman's last month and some of the coral had broken away from the hurricane winds. I got permission to collect it. Mom has a jeweler that she has used for years and he crafted it into a necklace and earrings for me to give to you. What do you think?"

She looked at him with large round eyes and said, "Oh Grey, it's beautiful. I love that you collected it and then had it made for me. You and the Caribbean will be with me always." What a special thing for him to do.

Grey said, "Here let me help you get the necklace on." He slipped the necklace on and his hands touched her neck when he was latching it. She savored his warm touch. After he was done fastening the necklace, she put on the drop-style French wire earrings. They were lightweight, but touched the side of her neck and face when she turned her head. She would wear these earrings and necklace and think of Grey's hand touching her.

Grey leaned down and pressed his open, wet lips to the tender skin on the back of her neck. "I've been thinking about you wearing this necklace and the earrings." He turned her to face him and smiled. His eyes darkened and his face got serious. He leaned in to kiss her tenderly on the mouth. "What I meant to say is that I've been thinking about you wearing this necklace and the earrings. Nothing else." His voice was husky, full of need and desire.

Gretchen felt fire blossom at the juncture of her legs. What she thought was a deep ache for Greyson Maddock was nothing compared to what she felt now in his presence, listening to him say those words to her. Gretchen whispered against his lips and closed her eyes, "I can make that happen, Mr. Maddock."

Grey groaned. He stood, took her hand and pulled her to stand in front of him. There were so many things Grey wanted to tell Gretchen, but there were no words to describe what he was feeling. He decided to show her.

He started the conversation by slipping his hand inside the stiff collar of her olive button down shirt. The color did amazing things to her eyes, but he could do amazing things to her body. Grey slid his hands over her collarbones. She closed her eyes and moaned.

It felt like an eternity since he touched her. She reached up to begin unbuttoning her shirt for him. He slid the shirt off her shoulders. His mouth replaced his hands and he loved her skin with his tongue and lips. Gretchen couldn't stand this slow, delicious torture and she said as much.

Grey smiled and looked at her through hooded eyes. "Babe, I'm going to make you want me so much that you would do anything to have me inside you." Grey looked at her breasts. Her nipples drew into stiff peaks just from his gaze.

He freed them quickly from their red satiny cups and sighed when he held them captive in his capable hands. She remembered his self-control from when they were together last. He was an unselfish lover, taking for himself only after she had come three times. Even when he took for himself, it was pleasurable for her, too.

He fingered the coral necklace and then bent to take a nipple into his mouth. Grey loved the taste of her skin. He moved to the other one while sinking his fingers deep into her derrière. Gretchen was a soft and curvy woman. To be here with her in his mouth was heaven. And, it was only going to get better.

Grey slid his hands around to the front of her jeans and began to work them open. She stilled his hands with her own. Gretchen turned her back to him and pulled his hands around her to her breasts. She rubbed her body up and down his while he massaged her breasts. His fingers pulled and tugged on her nipples while she pressed against him.

His erection pressed against her bottom. The friction was delicious. He kissed the back of her neck and behind her ears. She stepped away from his embrace. She looked over her shoulder at him, seductively.

"I have a gift for you, too." Gretchen pushed her jeans down over her full hips. She knew Grey appreciated her female curves.

"Oh. My. God, Babe." Gretchen was wearing a red lace thong. Her smooth slightly tanned bottom begged to be touched, kissed, licked, held with his strong hands while he drove into her. Her long auburn hair was curly and fell almost to her waist.

His attention was drawn to the top of the thong. There was a darkening area just under the triangle of fabric. He reached to hook a finger under the edge. Grey was going to remove it since she would not have any need of it.

Grey's hand froze when he pulled the material away from her body. The darkened area was a tattoo that was about two inches long. It was a tattoo of a sailboat with the sails up. It was simple, but oh so sexy on her body.

She said, "It's for you. I always wanted a tattoo and I thought with the sailboat..." Gretchen's voice trailed off when she looked at Grey's face over her shoulder.

She was so stupid to think he would like that. "I can see that you don't really like it." Her heart sank.

Gretchen started to turn around to face him and Grey grabbed her to him. He whispered in her ear over her shoulder, "Babe, that's the sexiest thing anyone has ever done for me. I think the tat is sexy and I think you are the sexiest woman I've ever known. I never knew making love could be so intense. With you, it's like nothing I've ever experienced."

Grey's breathless comments were punctuated with kisses on her neck and back. He held her with one hand on her breast while he kissed her. He quickly unzipped his jeans and pushed them to the floor to join her clothes. One benefit of going commando was that he was ready for Gretchen at anytime.

He stripped his shirt off so they could be skin on skin. He pressed his firm, throbbing need against her. With the free hand, he reached around to the place where she wanted him to touch. She moaned when his fingers slid between her wet, thick folds and found her most sensitive bud. He circled it with his finger while he pinched her nipple. She almost came undone. It felt so good.

She pushed against his hardness thinking about it being inside of her. Grey was right, she would do anything to have him inside her. He slid one, then two fingers inside her. She gasped. Grey's fingers were pure magic. He rubbed and circled her bud until her orgasm burst and spread all over her body. "Oh, Grey, I want you inside me now." His erection wept for her body.

He had to have her right then. He gently put his hand on her back and bent her over the couch so he could look at her gifts-the tattoo and her sweet behind. Quickly, he rolled on a condom. He slowly pushed himself deep into her. Grey fought the urge to drive into her with reckless abandon. It was Gretchen and the snug fit that made it even sweeter. Gretchen's moans reached his ears and he could no longer control it. He started pumping himself in and out of her.

He shuddered every time he entered her. He reached around to slide his fingers over her spot. She was slick with wanting him. She was so receptive to his touch. Gretchen whined, "Oh Grey, harder, please."   With one hand on her breast, twisting and tugging on her nipple and one magic finger rubbing her spot, Grey began to pound into her. As the pleasure built, Grey and Gretchen went higher and higher until they were both freefalling into earth-shattering bliss.

Their bodies spent with the passionate burst of lovemaking over the back of the couch, Gretchen lead him to her bedroom. They crawled under the warm down comforter. Grey held her close and played with her red curls that splayed over him and the pillows while she closed her eyes and breathed in his scent. Gretchen relished having him in her bed and snuggled closer to him.

He kissed the top of her head and said, "I'm looking forward to spending the whole weekend with your body. Five months is too long. I've really missed you."

"Oh really? I thought you were coming to see me because I was a great conversationalist." Gretchen wanted more than just a fabulous weekend with Grey. She didn't know how to communicate that to him. For some reason, she thought he might have commitment issues when it came to relationships. Surely he'd slept with someone else in the last five months. They hadn't discussed exclusivity in their relationship.

He used the tip of his finger to tilt her head up to look at him. "Yes, babe. That, too." Grey smiled and traced her lips with his fingers. They were so full and pouty and begged to be kissed. Gretchen read his mind as she slid her body up so that their lips could meet. The kiss was soft and gentle. He lifted her so that she was straddling him, her smooth legs on either side of his hips, her moist heat covering his growing erection.

Grey sat up with Gretchen astride him and laid her back. He moved so that he was over her and began suckling her nipple. His tongue trailed down her belly, pausing for a moment to flick it at her belly button ring.

He looked up at her and said, "This right here is a huge turn on. I was turned into flint instantly when I saw it the first time when we were down by the river." He bent his head to flick it again and then moved lower. When Gretchen realized what he meant to do, her stomach knotted up and she moaned closing her eyes.

Grey's warm breath hit her inner thighs in little bursts. He was almost panting. Grey looked at her for a moment and then said, "You are so wet for me. You're making my mouth water to taste you."

Gretchen was anticipating his mouth on her very sensitive tissues. "Grey, honey, stop using your mouth to talk." She was almost squirming under him. Grey looked up and cocked an eyebrow. A slow sexy grin that was almost evil spread across his face. "My pleasure, babe." She knew the pleasure would be all hers.

She watched his brown wavy head dip between her legs. When his hot tongue touched her, it burned pleasantly. She gasped and her hips bucked. Grey reached up to tweak a nipple while he made slow love to her with his mouth. "Mmm, babe. You taste so good." When she was fully aroused, he did this lick-suck-flick thing with his tongue that did her in. Grey Maddock was a brilliant lover.

Grey entered her slowly. She tightened around him and he sucked in a breath. He'd never felt anything so intense, so deep in his soul, so much like love. Yes, he loved her. He knew that the moment she came against his mouth; no, he knew a long time before that. Grey loved being the man to make her feel good. He wanted to be the only one. She was his.

Grey and Gretchen made love this time in her bed and without the feverish pace. It was achingly sweet. They came together and then drifted off to sleep. Grey snuggled up behind her and rested his thumb on her belly ring.

Chapter Eight

The phone was ringing. Gretchen awoke and the room was dark except for a soft glow from the nightlight in her bathroom. She glanced at the clock. 7:18 p.m.

She and Grey had drifted off to sleep after their lovemaking. She reached over him to get the phone. As she answered, she saw the covers had slipped from him and his muscular behind was demanding her attention. She reached out and grabbed it as she said, "Hello?"

"Hi, Gretchen?" She recognized tension in the voice on the other end of the line. It was Marianne.

Jeb.

"Yes? Marianne? What's wrong?" Gretchen immediately was alert. Marianne was with Jeb and the scouts at the retreat. Grey heard the alarm in her voice and sat straight up in the bed placing a hand on the small of her back. He was listening to Gretchen's side of the conversation.

"Jeb fell out of a tree and I think he might have broken his arm. He's having some trouble moving his fingers and the arm looks bent in a funny spot. He's doing just fine otherwise. He has ice on it and I've given him some over-the-counter pain reliever. " Marianne, bless her heart, was trying to do damage control. She didn't want to worry Gretchen, but knew Jeb needed to be taken to the hospital for an x-ray.

"Marianne, I will be there in about twenty-five minutes. Can you tell Jeb that?" Gretchen knew it would take about that long for her to get dressed and drive to the retreat site.

"Of course. Drive carefully and I'll see you in a little while." Marianne hung up and Gretchen flew out of the bed and started throwing on some clothes. Grey looked at her waiting for her explanation to what was going on.

"Babe, what's happened? Do you want me to go with you?" He stood with his arms out oblivious to his nakedness. Grey's hair was rumpled and he had a line on his face from her pillowslip. He was perfect and Gretchen really wanted to crawl back into his arms.

"That was Marianne at the retreat site and Jeb fell out of a tree. She thinks his arm might be broken." She was looking around for a pair of socks. "No, I'll go alone. I didn't mention to Jeb you were coming here this weekend." Gretchen didn't want to look Grey in the eye. Grey didn't know how he felt about her not sharing with Jeb that he was coming to visit.

"Were you going to tell him I was here to see you?" Grey wanted to know. He immediately felt odd for being in Missouri and in Gretchen's bed naked. Grey waited for her answer and when it didn't come, he went to the living room to get his jeans. He walked back into the bedroom with his jeans unbuttoned and a dark thatch of hair showing. "Well, were you?" He was trying to keep his temper under control.

Gretchen needed to get to Jeb. "Yes, Grey, I was going to tell him after I saw how this weekend went. He doesn't know anything about us. I haven't told him how we met in New Orleans and that we've been emailing and calling back and forth. He's a ten-year-old little boy that has been through enough. Can we have this discussion after I have Jeb's arm seen about?" She gathered her jacket and pair of tennis shoes out of the closet.

"What if I'm not here when you get back? Maybe it's not a good idea that Jeb see me here with his Mom." The hurt was showing in his voice.

Gretchen had been rushing around to find her car keys. She stopped what she was doing and turned to face him. "Grey, don't leave. Please be here when we get back. I will talk to Jeb and then we'll be home. You and I will get this straightened out."

"Gretchen, I don't think there's anything to straighten out. I have nearly bared my soul to you and you haven't even mentioned to your son that we are in a relationship?" He was getting angry. She couldn't have this discussion now.

"Grey, I didn't want him to know you until I knew it was a stable relationship that might last. It's not fair to him and I don't want him to think that his mother is just dating around with different men." Gretchen reached out her hand to touch him.

Grey moved away from her. "When you have the courage to tell your son that you have another man in your life that's not him or his Daddy, then you give me a call." He picked up his shirt and slid it over his head.

"Please, Grey, don't leave me. Be here when I get back. " Gretchen was pleading and she had very little time. She knew Jeb would be waiting.

"It's not likely to happen." Grey wouldn't even look at her. He stood with his back to her. She stared at that strong, broad back and remembered how the muscles shifted and felt under her touch.

She shut her eyes tight and swallowed the lump forming in her throat. She paused with her hand on the door and her back to Grey. Her voice was low and shaky, "Grey, for what it's worth, I think I am in love with you." Gretchen quietly closed the door behind her.

Grey turned to address Gretchen's statement with a shocked look on his face. She was already gone. The house was quiet. The scent of Gretchen and their lovemaking remained faintly in the air. Grey said out loud to the empty house, "Maddock, you've done it again." He sunk into her couch and put his head in his hands. Grey knew he loved Gretchen and to leave now wouldn't be a good demonstration of that fact.

Chapter Nine

The tears started falling and didn't stop until she reached the turn off for the retreat site. As she drove her car, her mind wound down narrow dark paths of hurt, loss and desperation. She was surprised at Grey's response. She really thought there was more to the relationship than sex. Gretchen couldn't get her mind around how hurt and shocked his voice sounded.

Gretchen should have known it wouldn't work out. Grey didn't have any children and couldn't understand what she needed to do. He didn't seem to want to understand. The hurt look on his face shredded Gretchen's heart. She loved the man, but she couldn't be with him if he was going to be so irrational when it came to Jeb. Gretchen was his mother and she alone was the one to decide what was best for them. For a man to have so much respect and love for his own mother, it was difficult to believe that he couldn't transfer those feelings.

Maybe Grey was just continuing the fling from New Orleans. She thought they were closer than just a fling, but what did she know? She knew the sex was over the top. She knew that the emails and phone calls seemed sincere and caring. She knew he was here, but he was here on business, too. Gretchen thought maybe she was just a convenience.

She didn't want to be a convenience. She had been there and done that and had a Diet Coke on the way.

Right now she had to see about Jeb and call his father to let him know what was going on. As she pulled into the site, Jeb came out to the car and met her with tears, "Mommy. I hurt my arm." Gretchen melted and put her arms gingerly around her son. She kissed his head and comforted him while Marianne loaded his pack in the trunk of Gretchen's car.

Gretchen comforted Jeb and settled him in the car with his ice pack. She turned to Marianne and hugged her. "Thank you for taking care of my baby." She smiled and said she would let the leaders know what the doctor said. Marianne waved them off and they headed for the hospital.

On the way, Gretchen dialed Jacob's cell phone. It rang twice and a female voice answered, "Hello?" She thought something about the voice was familiar but she was in no frame of mind to investigate. She didn't really care who was answering her ex-husband's phone; she just needed to talk to him.

"This is Gretchen. May I talk to Jake?" Gretchen waited for the voice's response.

"Oh, hi Gretchen. Jake's still at the store, can I give him a message?" The voice was saccharine and Gretchen was puzzled.

"Yes, please tell him that Jeb fell out of a tree at the scout retreat and I am taking him to North Memorial for an x-ray. His arm does appear to be broken." Gretchen was trying to relay all the important information in hopes it would get to his dad.

"Well, Gretchen, you don't know if it's broken until they x-ray it, right? Why don't you just call back and let me know what the x-rays show and if it's broken, I'll let Jaykie know and we'll come out to the hospital. They got a big wholesale truck in late this afternoon and there's no sense in bothering him for no reason." The voice was speaking down to Gretchen.

Gretchen's temper raised a notch. Jaykie? Three letters came to mind that she and Lou used a lot when they would text message each other: WTF? "Excuse me, to whom am I speaking?" Her Jeb who didn't miss anything, looked at her and rolled his eyes. She glanced at him and shrugged her shoulders.

"It's Jean. Jean Willoughby. "

The name rang a bell. There were so many names and faces in her head it was like a Rolodex the size of a Ferris wheel. How many Jeans did she know? Jean Willoughby.

Oh. My. Gosh. It was Jean Byers. The Jean from high school that Jake's father liked because they went to church together. She was such a floozy then and still sounded like one on the phone. Guess it was one of those things you don't outgrow.

Jean had married Kyle Willoughby right out of high school. Kyle, the football captain in high school, turned out to be a gold digger and an alcoholic. He gambled and drank away all of Jean's inheritance from her father. Jean's father had been injured while working for the railroad and had received a large settlement.

Jean didn't go to college after high school because she depended on her father's money to take care of her. The rumor was she was back in town and broke. Now, Gretchen realized who she was. Why was she answering her ex-husband's phone and screening his calls?

"Yes, I remember you now. Some things never change. Look, Jean, he would want to know that his child has been injured. Give him the message as soon as we hang up." Gretchen closed her flip phone.

She was boiling. How dare that woman be the one to decide if Jake was coming to see about his son or not! That was Jake's decision, not hers. She hoped her fury was well masked with concern over Jeb's arm. It wasn't.

"It was Jean wasn't it, Mom?" Jeb looked at her and read her every emotion no matter how hard she tried to conceal them from him. Gretchen was shocked to hear Jeb's question.   "Yes, honey, but how did you know?" Gretchen was now curious as they pulled under the lights of the North Memorial parking lot. It was full as usual on a Friday night.

Jeb rolled his eyes. "She's been out there helping Dad with the bookwork the last month or so. She's even got some soap and shampoo in his bathroom. I guess it's there for when she gets dirty from shelving stuff. Sometimes it feels like she lives there. It's kind of weird." Bless Jeb's innocence. Gretchen's stomach lurched. She immediately got control of the nausea and thought to herself it was unfair for her to be with someone else and not expect Jake to do the same.

Thing is, Jake probably wasn't the one doing the pursuing. Gretchen was sure Jean's predatory instincts kicked in and she was on the prowl. These days, Jean only cared if a man had a house, a nice truck and health insurance. It didn't matter to her if the guy was into her or not as long as he told her how beautiful she was and that she smelled nice. He also had to have a fat wallet to take care of her since Kyle had literally drunk and pissed away her bankroll. Jean was accustomed to someone taking care of her. Jean didn't have a father, a brother, or a clue.

Gretchen went to retrieve a wheelchair to transport Jeb inside. She thought riding in the wheelchair might be more comfortable for him and not bump his arm around too much. Besides, he was her star and she wanted to focus on him. Gretchen helped Jeb into the chair and shut and locked the doors of her Civic. It chirped back at her and they wheeled up to the Emergency Department entrance.

Jeb benefited from having a mom as a nurse in some medical facilities. This was one of those facilities. When the clerk saw Gretchen pushing him in the door, the other non-emergency frequent flyers took a backseat.

Stan, a male nurse whom Gretchen had gotten acquainted with many years ago in nursing school greeted them. "Hey, what's hanging with you all tonight? Did you come by to see me?" Stan smiled and winked at Gretchen. Stan was a nice man who was married with two kids and a dog.

"No, Mr. Stan. I think the ground got the best of Jeb's arm when he fell out of a tree at the scout retreat earlier this evening." Gretchen continued to follow Stan back to the curtained area where patients were being evaluated. Jeb was comfortable with the staff at North Memorial because his mother had worked with many of them throughout the years of her nursing career.

"I was chasing a lizard up the tree. I just knew I could catch him. The next thing I knew, there were some cracking sounds and then I'm on the ground. My arm was between the big limb and the ground." Jeb was excited relaying his side of the story to Stan and the attending physician. Dr. Huntz was new to North Memorial ER. Stan quickly explained how he knew Gretchen and Jeb.

"Jeb. How about we go and get a picture of your arm and see what's really going on?" Dr. Huntz was explaining to Jeb about the x-ray and what to expect. All things he thought he already knew.

"Look doc, my mom is a nurse and she's pretty smart. She's told me all this stuff before so can we just get this show on the road? I have some badges to earn at scout retreat." Jeb was all business when it came to earning his badges and awards with scouts.

Embarrassed, Gretchen scolded Jeb by giving him The Look and apologized to Dr. Huntz. "I'm so sorry for his rudeness. He is just excited about the retreat. Do what you need to do, please."

Dr. Huntz stepped closer to Gretchen and lowered his voice. She felt a little like a young female cat cornered by a Tom Cat. "I can't do what I need to do in front of all these people. How 'bout you give me your number and I'll call you later?" He smiled big showing his horse teeth. She raised her eyebrows.   What in the world?

For a moment Gretchen was speechless. Then looked him straight in the eye. With fists on her hips she said, "How about you just x-ray his arm and bill the insurance?" She was nice, but firm and her body language spoke volumes.

Dr. Huntz stared at her for a moment, amused. "Whatever you wish, ma'am." He turned on his heel and headed to x-ray. He whistled a tune while he danced down the hallway.

Stan hid his smile behind Jeb's chart. Gretchen elbowed him in the ribs. "Ouch. Why did you do that?" His question was punctuated with spurts of laughter.

"That's for not rescuing me. What was *that*?" The new doctor was giving her the creeps. As long as he knew how to effectively and correctly read an x-ray, she could deal with his untoward advance.

"Oh, I think he's harmless. I think he is just looking for some companionship. He really has been nailing the diagnoses, though. I think he's a decent doc." Stan was still chuckling.

"That's a relief. I would be really disturbed if he came on to me and screwed up Jeb's arm." Gretchen paced until they returned from x-ray. She worried about Jeb. She wondered if Jean had given Jacob the message. She wondered if she would still have a visitor when she got home.

Whistling could be heard in the distance. As Dr. Huntz and Jeb got closer to the ED, it got louder. "It's definitely broken. Luckily Jeb did it right." He handed Gretchen the film to look at. "It's a good clean linear break. We're going to send him home in a soft cast tonight to let the swelling go down. He needs to see the bone doc on Monday for re-evaluation. They will probably cast it then, if the swelling has resolved enough to be appropriate to cast." Dr. Huntz was handing the prescriptions for pain to Gretchen and they were just getting ready to head out the door. "Until then, rest and ice and take the pain meds. No climbing trees or chasing lizards." Dr. Huntz pointed at Jeb and winked.

"Hey buddy." It was Jake's voice. I guess he had gotten the message after all. A little late as usual, but he had made it. It only took about seven minutes to get to North Memorial from Jake's store. Gretchen and Jeb had been there for almost an hour and a half. He came up and ruffled his hair. "Is it broken?" Jake addressed the doctor instead of his ex-wife.

Dr. Huntz looked at Gretchen. "I was just telling his Mom that it is broken, but it's the best kind of break to have." Dr. Huntz droned on about the follow up appointment and the medicine for Jeb.

Gretchen hadn't seen Jacob in awhile except from the shoulders up in the truck. When he came for Jeb, he would pull up and honk and Jeb would come out. He hadn't been inside the house since the divorce.

Jake didn't look so good. He had lost weight, his jeans were baggier than usual and there were dark circles under his hollow blue eyes. There was no one at home to cook for him and take care of him anymore. Gretchen never noticed how gray his hair had gotten. He looked like an old man.

Gretchen felt partially responsible for his appearance. She was no longer married to him and didn't have to feel that way, but she did. She loved Jacob Mitchell and always would. He was the father of her child. Maybe he really did love me but couldn't find a way to show me? She talked to herself barely moving her lips as she looked at the man she used to share a bed and a life with. "Doesn't matter. What's done is done. I'm happy and I'm going to move on. "

"Jaaayyyykie." The voice was like chewing on a silver gum wrapper with fillings in your teeth. Painful. Unnerving. A glimpse of Jean Willoughby was caught through the door as Gretchen looked toward the sound. She must have followed Jacob to the hospital. "I want to know what's going on with my step-son!" Her shout brought the hairs up on Gretchen's neck and caused Jake and Jeb to blush.

It wasn't that she was shouting. It was what she said. Gretchen craned her neck to glare at Jake. She took him by the arm and they stepped out of the curtained area into a small closet of medical supplies. "What's this malarkey about Jean and her 'step-son'?"

Gretchen was livid. Her face was red and her eyes were wild. If he was serious with someone, she felt like he owed it Jeb to let him know. If he had wed behind their son's back, there would be hell to pay and she was the collector.

"Well, Gretchen, you look good, but you can just calm down." Jake spread his hands out in front of her, palms down. She absolutely despised when he said that. He was looking at her like she might totally lose it. "Don't throw bags of fluids at me or anything." Gretchen rolled her eyes. She wasn't that upset. Ok, so maybe she was.

It wouldn't be the IV fluid bags though. It would be the intramuscular injection syringes. Their needles were long and big and strong and they could be more accurate. Gretchen smiled. Like darts.

She was always good at throwing darts. She looked at Jake and imagined a giant dartboard on his butt. He was running and screaming and she was throwing IM syringes at him. Gretchen started to giggle. The giggle turned into a full-blown laugh. Jake looked at her and started to inch out of the supply closet.

"Oh no you don't, mister. You are not off the hook. Tell me about Jean." Gretchen stood there with the hands on her hips and her eyes sparking. Jake had a fleeting thought of the flammable alcohol in the closet and the fire in her eyes. He didn't want this to be any worse than it already was going to be.

"Gert, honey, let me explain." Jake started to do just that when she stopped him with a palm in his face.

"Don't 'Gert' me, Jacob. Spill it. Short and sweet. I've ridden the emotional rollercoaster long enough tonight." She briefly thought of how her late afternoon started by making love with Grey and how far she'd ridden to get to the point of standing in a medical supply closet with her ex-husband while a floozy called him 'Jaykie' in public. She also noticed Jake eyeing her necklace that Grey had given her with curiosity. How dare he use his pet name on her.

"Ok." Jake sighed. "Jean called me when she got back to town and said her Momma had told her I was divorced and she started coming around. I like her and so we are getting married next weekend. That's it; short and sweet." It all came out in a rush. Jake winced and ducked his head. He thought the medical supply assault would now begin.

When it didn't, he straightened and opened one eye to look at Gretchen.

One bark of laughter left Gretchen's mouth. She stood in front of Jacob Mitchell at a loss for words and her hand over her mouth. Today she had been speechless more than once. Finally, she found her voice. Her eyes were large circles in her pale face. Quietly she asked while looking at him through narrowed eyes, "Do you love her?"

Jake moved closer to her and put both hands on her shoulders. He shook his head. "Aw Gretchen. Love is no longer, well... We are just two people who are going to try to make a life together. Don't make it more complicated than it is." This was the reason, formed into words she had left him. He didn't feel passionately about anyone but himself and his hardware store. Maybe his son, Jeb, had his love. It wasn't that he was selfish, although it would seem that way. He was an only child and didn't know how to think of anything other than himself. It was a pitiful excuse, but there it was. And, sadly Gretchen was relieved.

For some strange reason, Gretchen felt a weight was lifted from her chest. She hugged his neck quickly and said, "Thank you. Oh, and you are the one telling your son." Jake nodded with a bewildered look on his face. Gretchen felt like she had been set free.

Someone was going to take care of Jake. She did want him to be happy. Maybe the floozy Jean could do that. Maybe he and Jean *were* meant for each other all along. Maybe someone had accidently poked Gretchen with a dose of morphine. Good gracious, she had to get out of here!

Successfully avoiding Dr. Huntz, Gretchen helped Jeb walk out of the hospital. Jean did get to come back and see Jeb on the condition that she never referred to him as her stepson.

Gretchen glanced over at Jeb in the dashboard lights on the way home. He had fallen asleep after taking his pain medicine in the ED. He would be a chunk to pack in the house. She'd done it before and would do it again.

She pulled into the driveway. It was empty and the porch light was left on. She sighed and turned off the car. As she gathered her things, she let Jeb sleep in the car until all of his camping stuff was in the house.

As she came out the front door to haul Jeb to his bed, she met Grey with her son in his arms. "He's quite a load, babe. Do you mind to get the door?" Gretchen was surprised to see Greyson Maddock standing on her porch with her son in his arms. His voice jolted her to action.

She opened the door and said, "Thank you for getting him. He is so heavy. With the medicine they gave him for pain, I knew he would be dead weight." She followed Grey to Jeb's room. The bed was already turned back and his TV was on. Gretchen kissed her son's cheek and took his shoes off and covered him up.

Grey watched while leaning against the doorframe. She was such an amazing woman. He knew he acted irrationally earlier. He jumped to a conclusion that wasn't true. He and Gretchen had some things to talk about.

Chapter Ten

Gretchen softly closed Jeb's door. She came into the kitchen where Grey was rattling around. He was making some hot tea for the two of them. She would have preferred something stronger, but maybe that wasn't best for the discussion that was inevitable.

"Babe, I'm sorry for my harsh actions and words earlier. I guess my feelings were hurt. I want to talk about why you didn't want to tell Jeb about us." Grey faced her and leaned his hips against the counter with his arms crossed over his chest. He had put a sweater on over his t-shirt that made him look so warm and cuddly. She would have to put her libido on hold and focus on the conversation.

"Grey, where are we on this 'us' thing? I don't want to tell Jeb that I have a man in my life that I care about and it not be leading to something serious. I feel like there is more to this friendship." What she said was honest, but she didn't really know how he felt.

Grey dropped his head and supported his weight by putting his hands on the counter behind him. What he was feeling was something serious. He looked up at her. "Gretchen, it's not up to me where we are on the 'us' thing. I think we are more than just friends with benefits. I care about you a great deal, but I don't want to just talk to you on the phone and on the computer. I want you in my life. Did you mean what you said before you walked out the door tonight?" The intensity in his eyes confirmed what he was saying with his lips.

Those lips. She had to kiss them. Gretchen wrapped her arms around Grey's neck and pressed her lips to his. She wanted to believe him. "I want to believe what you are telling me. I also want you to believe that I am falling in love with you. I know it sounds unreal, but it's how I feel."

Grey wrapped his arms around her and put his chin on her head. He took a deep breath and sighed. "Believe me, Babe, I am falling in love with you, too. Why don't you and Jeb come down over Christmas and meet my Mom and I'll show you my home place?"

Gretchen leaned back to look at him. She grinned and asked, "Do you really mean it?" The thought of going to St. Bart's to see him and meet his mom was very exciting. He had also invited her son, which made her ecstatic.

"Of course I mean it. I want you and Jeb to come down. I have some frequent flyer miles and you and Jeb can use those." He had given it some thought while she went to get Jeb and have his arm evaluated. He had done some evaluating on his own.

Grey was excited about having her on his turf. Maybe if she came for a visit, then she would be more motivated to find a way to stay with him on his island.

"Alright. I will see what we can arrange. " She began to smile and nod. About that time, she heard Jeb's door open. He trudged into the bathroom and closed the door.

She made her way to the hall. "Jeb, honey, are you okay?" Gretchen was at the bathroom door. She heard the toilet flush and Jeb opened the door. He stood in the hall a little foggy eyed and looked over her shoulder at Grey.

Grey waved at Jeb and said, "Hi, Jeb. I'm Grey Maddock. I'm in love with your mother and I'm here to see her this weekend. Hopefully you and I will get a chance to get to know each other." The silence made Grey and Gretchen uncomfortable. "Hey, Dude. Whatever. I'm going back to bed. Can we talk about this in the morning?" Jeb turned and shuffled to his bedroom without waiting for their reply. After he closed his door, they turned and looked at each other.

"That wasn't so bad. Maybe the pain medicine took the edge off." Gretchen grinned and shrugged. She had expected more drama. Maybe after a good night's rest they could all sit down and talk.

"I don't want it this way, but I think it's best if you sleep in the guest room for now." Gretchen helped him with his things and turned back the bed in the guest room. "There are towels and washcloths in the basket by the tub. If you need anything else, let me know or please, help yourself."

She hugged and kissed Grey goodnight and closed the door to her bedroom. For now, it was best to keep the appearance that they were not sleeping together in front of Jeb. Those were private moments for her and Grey.

She rolled over to look at the clock. 3:39 a.m. and she still hadn't fallen asleep. Gretchen kept thinking about Grey being under her roof and she was in her bedroom alone. She got up and went in the `living room`.

There was Grey on the couch in flannel pants with the remote control in his hand. He had his reading glasses on trying to figure out how to change the channels. She walked over to the couch and sat down beside him. "Need some help, sailor?" She smiled at him and took in his wonderful chest and the vision he made on her couch.

He smiled back at her. Grey put his arm around her, placing his hand on her bottom when she tucked into the crook of his arm and leaned on his strong chest. Grey relinquished the remote. Her hair tickled his skin although she had it in a ponytail. He closed his eyes and thought of her hair on her pillow and on him. Neither of them talked about how they were going to make this very long distance relationship work.

Chapter Eleven

Grey and Gretchen awoke to Jeb standing in front of them, bundled in his quilt. The morning sun was shining through the French Doors behind the couch and the TV was set on VH-1. Grey and Gretchen had used a throw as a cover and it had slipped to the floor. Grey leaned to retrieve it to cover Gretchen. He was pretty sure they were both clothed appropriately, but he wasn't for certain.

"So, what's for breakfast?" Jeb was usually hungry and he loved breakfast. He stood in the living room yawning and stretching. He reached over to pick up the remote from the floor and switched the channel to cartoons.

"Are you hurting this morning, Bub?" Gretchen was concerned about Jeb's arm. He had slept all night.

Jeb looked down at his arm. "Naw. It's not too bad."

Gretchen just smiled and thought that morning was going normal and weird all at the same time. She expected Jeb to be upset that his mother had fallen asleep with a strange man on the couch. He wasn't. Jeb was only hungry.

Grey clapped his hands and rubbed them together. He gathered the reading glasses from the table and stuck them in the brown curls on his head. "Hey Jeb. Do you like pancakes? I have a great homemade pancake recipe."

Jeb's eyes got huge. He nodded enthusiastically and smiled. "Can I help you make them?" Jeb loved to help Gretchen in the kitchen. He was her little chef. The two of them cooking in the kitchen was going to make a mess.

"Absolutely. Why don't you let your beautiful mom jump in the shower and we'll get breakfast started. Sound good to you, Gretchen?" Grey looked at Gretchen and winked.

Gretchen looked at Grey standing in the living room with his soft pants, his brown broad shoulders and the dusting of light, sun-kissed hair on his chest. Pants she had been able to manage. She warmed at the thought of what had happened on the couch last night. She couldn't get enough of Grey Maddock. "Yep. Sounds good to me. Then we'll get our day started." Gretchen headed off for her room to shower.

Grey and Jeb made a huge mess in her kitchen making the most delicious pancakes. Both of them cleaned it up while she sat on the swing on the front porch drinking a cup of coffee. She made a phone call to Marianne to let her know that Jeb's arm was broken, but they didn't think surgery was going to be necessary. She also explained that Jeb wouldn't be back to camp for the weekend.

The three of them loaded up in Gretchen's car with Grey driving. Grey didn't have any idea where he was going, but being a man's man, he wanted to drive . She gave him directions and about an hour later they wound up at Elephant Rocks State Park.

Jeb loved to play in this park. It had large rocks to climb on and around and trails to walk. Gretchen had spent several hours here with Jeb. Gretchen wanted Grey to see something in Missouri that he wouldn't see on St. Barts. Gretchen had packed a picnic lunch while the boys showered. She lifted the basket out of the backseat while Grey retrieved the cooler from the trunk.

They all sat and ate at a table in the shade. The sun was warm and the breeze was cool and fresh. It was a perfect autumn day. Gretchen smiled and turned her face to the sun. Jeb couldn't stop asking Grey questions about sailing and St. Barts. Grey couldn't stop asking questions about scouting and school. Finally Grey said, "I've invited you and your mother to the island over Christmas. Do you think you would like that?"

Jeb sat thoughtful for a moment. "Well, what about my Dad? What will he do at Christmas? I know that he and Jean will be together, but I don't know if I want to be away from my Dad for Christmas." He looked pained as if he had to decide that day on his own. Jeb looked up at his mother.

Gretchen smiled and rubbed his head and neck, then drew him close to her body. "We don't have to decide today, Jeb. We will talk to your Dad about Christmas. We will work something out that will make everyone happy." She knew the holidays were going to be rough for everyone. Jeb also had a birthday coming up in December. The first one with divorced parents. Her stomach turned over.

The weekend ended much too soon and Grey was putting his things into the rental. He told Gretchen he would call her when he got to the airport. He hugged and kissed her in front of her son. Shaking Jeb's hand he said, "Thanks for letting me hang out with you and your Mom this weekend. Take care of her until I see you both again." Jeb smiled at Grey and nodded.

Grey got in the car and Gretchen leaned her head in the open window to kiss him one last time. "Until

December." She smiled at him, told him to call her, and then he was backing down the driveway. She stood behind Jeb with her elbows resting on his shoulders. It wouldn't be long before she wouldn't be able to do that anymore. When did Jeb get this tall? "Well, what do you think?"

"Mom, I like him. I think he's a nice guy and he knows how to sail. I think he would be a neat step-dad." Jeb turned and went into the house.

Gretchen stood there like a stone letting Jeb's words sink in. She began to smile and the smile grew bigger. She thought to herself, yes he would and he would make a fabulous husband.

Chapter Twelve

Back on the island, his mother had watched him work and observed a difference in him. Clare Maddock was a bold woman who had always been an inspiration and source of strength for him. His mom was also like cheap toilet paper-she didn't take crap off anyone. Clare wasn't one to beat around the bush. She walked into his office and asked, "Who is she?"

Grey looked up from his desk. His mother didn't miss anything. He knew that his happiness showed on his face and in his voice. "Whatever do you mean, Mother?" Grey said with a teasing smile.

"Greyson Michael Maddock. You might fool some other old broad, but you don't fool me. I'm your mother, remember?" She stood with her hands on her hips. The same green eyes that Greyson saw reflected in the morning mirror stared back at him with a twinkle. Her skin was tough and wrinkled from all the time in the sun and the weather. Grey should claim responsibility for some of those wrinkles. He had taken a toll on her, too. The lines grew in a pleasant way as she smiled bigger at him.

Grey knew from a very young age that when she used his middle name, he better respond or act appropriately. He waited just a moment longer to draw out her suspense. He put his pen down and looked his mother in the face. He tented his fingers in front of his face. "OK. If you must know, I met a woman whose name is Gretchen when I was in New Orleans. She is a nurse and lives in Missouri. She is divorced and has a ten-year-old son named Jeb. We have been emailing each other the last five months, and calling the last six weeks or so. When I was in St. Louis talking with the brewery execs, I rented a car and went to see her. I also met Jeb and I really like him. Good kid." Grey waited for his mother's reply.

"Do I get to meet her and her son or are you going to continue to keep them a secret?" Clare Maddock never stopped being his mother although he was 42 years old. She needed to put her eyes on the woman to see if she was good enough for her son. Grey needed a special someone in his life. Clare had been blessed to have his dad.

Clare had tried to convince Grey the first time around that Kate Fisher wasn't good for him, but he was not thinking with his brain. Even his own mother knew it was a much lower part of his anatomy that was making his decisions in those days. She thought he might be a little more insightful this time.

"Well, maybe. She is really busy with her work and Jeb's schedule of scouting and school activities. She would really like to come down. I've invited her and Jeb down for Christmas." He continued to look and his mother.

"Are you going to marry her?" His mother could always get him to thinking about things he didn't want to think about.

The question made Grey smile. He had thought of that. Waking up to Mrs. Gretchen Maddock had its appeal. She really liked her job and he supposed that technically she could work from St. Barts. Where would Jeb stay? That would be the thing that kept Gretchen from making the Caribbean her home and he couldn't ask her to leave her son.

He turned in his chair to stare out the window at the bay. He studied the boats bobbing against the dock. He felt like that sometimes, bobbing along through life. His parents were the like the bumpers on the boats and the dock. They were there to keep him from being injured when terrible memories came at him like a hurricane.

"Mom, I have thought about that, but don't know how it would work with her son. I do know that I really like talking to her and she makes me feel, oh I don't know, human and loveable again."

Grey's mother came around the desk and put her arms around his neck over the back of his chair. "Grey honey. What happened with your father was not your fault. You have to quit blaming yourself for that. He was a victim of circumstances. I could have been the one with him instead of you." She kissed the top of his head in an effort to soothe him. In her mind, he would never cease to be her three-year-old child that needed his mother.

"Mom, you and I both know that I could have prevented the accident. I miss Dad so much. It was my carelessness and haste that killed him. If I hadn't had to have things my way . . ." Tears threatened to spill from Grey's green eyes just remembering that horrible day.

Greyson Maddock, Sr. had always felt when it was his time to go, it was his time to go. It didn't matter if he was wearing a seat belt or a life jacket. When his number was up, that was it. He would be put in for a celestial transfer. Grey was there when the day arrived.

Grey remembered the day all too well. He had just finished working on his own sailboat made from wood. He was so excited at his achievement. His father had explained that he needed to caulk the wood and let it dry before he went out for his maiden voyage.

The hull was made with planked plywood and caulked and although that was a strong hull, they did tend to leak if they weren't maintained. Also when not constructed properly, the laminated edges could separate and water would leak into the vessel. Grey had not worked on very many vessels like this one.

His father kept saying to him, "Son, caulking is a very important step in maintaining your vessel. So is patience. I don't want all your hard effort to go to waste. It could leak; take on water when you are out at sea. It could sink off the shores of one of those little uninhabited islands from which you love to spear fish." Grey knew his dad had a point, but he was anxious to take her out. Even at twenty-nine, his headstrong attitude was going to prevail.

"Dad, it will be fine. I'm not going far and I'll take a radio." Grey quickly gathered his fishing supplies and a beach towel. He grabbed the radio on the way out, but never paused to check the radar. He only looked at the skies and thought they were blue with a few fair-weather cumulus clouds. The water was calling to him and he didn't see the cumulonimbus clouds banking up. What kind of sailor doesn't check the weather before sailing?

A nasty storm blew up about fifteen minutes into his fishing trip. The thunderstorm blew his schooner about on the waves. A large wave came up and tossed him overboard. Grey was barely able to get back on board and pull up the anchor. He barely had a chance to put on his life jacket before a wave broadsided the schooner and nearly ousted him again.

His plans were to beach the boat and take shelter on the island under a tree or in a cave until the storm passed. The rain was pelting his head and the hail was biting into his skin. The radio would only crackle with the lightening strikes and he was not able to call out or hear anyone respond.

His dad arrived on a rescue boat shortly after Grey had made it to the island for cover. He came out in this beast of a storm because he knew that Grey would be in trouble. Shortly after his dad arrived, the boards on Grey's schooner started to split apart. He was grateful and aggravated to see his rescuer. "What in the hell do you think you are doing coming out in this?" Grey had to yell over the storm to talk to his dad. The rain continued to pour out of the black clouds of the sky. It sure didn't look like two o'clock in the afternoon.

"Whew! This sure is a booger of a storm. Makes me feel alive! I haven't been out in one of these since 1976. Have I told you about that?" His dad didn't seem the least bit worried about the storm or how they were going to get back home.

With a wild look in his eye he said to his son, "Sure am glad I kissed your momma before I left port. She was madder than a wet hen because you left and that I was goin' after you." He threw his had back and laughed as lightening struck and thunder boomed. Grey looked at his father like he was nuts.

"Dad, get under this tree. There is some protection from the storm here." Grey motioned for him to come and sit beside him. He had fashioned a little pallet out of palm fronds and the seat wasn't all that uncomfortable. It wasn't too bad once you were out of the storm.

Watching the power of Mother Nature had always been enthralling for the Maddock family. All they could do was wait it out. Grey's schooner was history; the hull was not even salvageable. Good thing his dad brought the fiberglass boat. Hopefully the motor wouldn't be too full of sand when the storm blew over.

"Ok, Dad, I'll bite. Tell me the story of 1976." Grey knew he was in for another tall tale. One never knew if their leg was being pulled with Greyson Maddock. He was always telling a story to be entertaining; they were mostly fiction inspired by some true events.

His dad laughed and slapped his knee. His face then got serious and he pointed his crooked, wrinkled finger in his son's face. "Now, if you ever tell your mother I told you this, I will say that you are lying. Remember the story I've told all these years about why I had to have stitches?"

Grey shook his head and looked at his father. "Dad, you've told this story to every fisherman and tourist. I've heard it at least forty times. Are you going to tell me that you weren't secretly watching a native islander initiation that went bad and ended with a homemade spear wound to your arm? It sounded really good and I think that's what you need to stick with. The tourists like it." Grey laughed and patted him on the back.

Greyson looked at his son with steel blue eyes that were very serious. He said, "Honestly son, that is not what happened. I had just bought a wood hulled boat that I patched myself and it was planked plywood. I had put the caulk on it and I was so impatient. Your mother was so worried about me taking it out and we had a huge fight about my safety."

He stopped talking and put his head down. Grey hadn't ever heard his parents fight or even argue. They were the best partners, working things out. He always thought his parents were the best Grey could imagine. They guided him to success but still allowed him to learn from his mistakes. He didn't want that illusion to shatter.

Taking a deep breath, his dad continued. "Well, I went out anyway just to show your mother. A storm blew up and my knockabout disintegrated. The caulk wasn't anywhere dry and the boards started leaking and then I could see the ocean under my boat. Luckily, I already had on my lifejacket and then bailed over the side, swimming towards the sand of an island.

"I had no idea where I was. The storm was much like this one. We had some serious weather and a couple of hurricanes that year and you know how that affects the ocean creatures and the climate of the water. What I didn't realize was that there was a pocket of very warm water close to the beach. There was a shelf where I could stand up about fifty feet out from the beach. The water hit me about the knee. I thought I was in good shape since I could stand up, but then when I started walking toward the beach, the shelf dropped back off.

"When the tide was in, two small sharks had found the drop off by accident because of the warmer water. They had been trapped there when the tide went out and it was too shallow for them to swim over the sandbar. I realized I had company after I felt one skin my leg. The water was murky from the storm and the sharks were as confused as I was about their location. They were hungry and I looked like dinner. It was very lucky that I only had thirty-seven stitches in my arm when my injuries could have been worse or I could have been eaten alive.

"Just because they were small didn't mean they didn't have teeth. It was hellish for a space of time that felt more like two days. The more I struggled to swim towards the shore, the harder they fought to eat me. I finally made it through the drop-off and onto the island.

"I lay there until the sun went down. The tide came up and the sharks were able to go back out to sea. By then, the storm had cleared and your mother had called for rescue knowing I needed help. I told her I was injured trying to save the knockabout. I couldn't tell her two sharks had attacked me. She would have never allowed me to sail again. It was my own stupidity and hard-headedness that got me into the mess. I asked the attending doctor to corroborate the story. He was also a sailor and understood my passion for it. He corroborated my story of the spear injury."

Grey was completely speechless as he stared at the man he called Dad. He had no idea what had really happened to his father to earn the thick, linear scar until today. He thought it was unlikely that he happened upon a native islander ritual. That story was almost funny. The truth scared Grey to death.

"Dad, I don't know what to say other than I'm sorry for not listening to you earlier today. I understand why you came out in this weather for me. You are a wise man and I have learned so much from you about sailing and life. You have always had my best interest at heart. You and Mom have always been the best parents a boy who is now a man could have. I love you." Grey couldn't stop the tears from falling. He knew what his father had risked coming out for him in this weather and the hell he must have been reliving. His Dad must have been worried sick about Grey to come out in the weather when it was so much like that fated day in 1976.

"I love you too, son. You've grown to be a fine young man with a smart head on those shoulders. You go and do whatever your heart desires. It's in you, son. Let's head home before your lovely mother makes me sleep in the office. I've grown accustomed to snuggling up to her at night and wouldn't want to ruin that chance." Grey's dad reached over and grabbed his shoulder and squeezed. He gave his son a smile and wink.

The weather was beginning to clear although thunder could still be heard and lightening seen in the distance. The rain had slowed to a drizzle and the wind had died down to a tropical breeze again. He and Grey got up to walk to the boat that his dad had beached. Hopefully they could get it started and back to port without too much of an incident.

Grey left out from under the palm tree first and headed to the boat. A streak of lightening came down from the sky and lit up the palm tree that his dad stood under. Grey remembered it happening in slowed time. His feet felt coated in drying cement and he couldn't make them move to get to him. He saw his father's face when the lightening struck.

He ran over and called to him, but his father wouldn't respond; he was not breathing on his own and Grey couldn't feel a pulse in his neck. The tree had caught fire and Grey pulled him away from the burning palm. Maybe the black smoke would signal someone to help him.

He had to try to revive his dad. Think Grey, think. He positioned his dad on his back with his head back to open his airway. How he remembered that, he had no idea. He raced to the rescue boat and located the radio. He carried that back along with a blanket, a towel, his father's SIG Sauer P229 Platinum Elite-being the eternal joker, he carried it in case of pirates-and a flare gun from the boat.

He tried the radio again. No luck. After that he began chest compressions and rescue breathing. He couldn't remember what the counts on each were but he thought anything would be better than nothing at all.

His dad was out here because of him. "Come on Dad, you can't leave us. We have to go fishing next Saturday." He would pump and breathe for his Dad some more. "Dad, come on, don't you leave me here. What if those sharks come back? I need you here." More chest compressions and breathing. Nothing was too much for the man who helped to give him life.

Like a miracle, the radio crackled to life. Grey was on the radio explaining where he was and that he had fired a flare from his location. He also explained excitedly to the dispatcher that his father was not breathing and had no heart rate. He also explained the lightening strike and that he was attempting CPR.

There was no response from his dad. He kept trying to compress and breathe but his emotions overcame him. His tears were blurring his vision and dripping onto his dad's chest and he felt so alone. He was angry and hurt that his dad would leave him and his mother. He was a five-year-old little boy again and he wanted his daddy back.

"Grey." His mother's voice brought him back to the office of GMS, Inc. "Your dad lived his life every day. He would want you to do the same. Your father always said when it was his time it was his time. Now, leave it at that."

Clare sighed deeply and came around in front of Grey to lean against his credenza. She looked at her son's face. "Honey, don't put your happiness on hold and say no to things because you feel guilty about what happened. We don't get too many chances in life to be happy. Gotta grab them when they present themselves. Your dad and I did. We went out on a limb to purchase the ships and open a business and never looked back, only forward. That's what you've got to do. Move forward. From what I can see, you are, and I want you to continue on that journey. I love you, son." Clare stood and motioned for her son to do the same. She gave him a big hug and motherly kiss on his mouth.

He hugged her back and then leaned to look down at Clare Maddock, "Mother, how do you know what I need when I need it?" Grey was amazed at his mother.

"Women have intuition. We just know things about the men we love." She smiled and opened her hands, palm up as a gesture of honesty. "So, when will they be here? Did you offer her the frequent flyer miles that we have racked up and never use around here?"

"Yes, Mom, I offered that to her. I am waiting to hear from Gretchen. She was going to talk to Jeb's dad about the days he wanted him and they would decide from there." As much as Grey wanted them both to come down, he also wanted to figure out a way to have some private time with Gretchen.

Clare sighed. "I suppose you will let me know in plenty of time to get food planned and gifts wrapped?" Her mind was already whirring to plan a family Christmas like they've not seen in the Maddock house in many years.

"Mom, do your worst!" Grey smiled as his mother shot a fist in the air and whooped out of the office. Even though she was fired up, she didn't look like herself. He shook his head. Right that moment he was determined to tell Gretchen the truth about his father's accident. Hopefully she would still love and accept him.

Chapter Thirteen

Gretchen's cell phone rang and the display showed 'Grey.' She welled with excitement at his unexpected call. "Grey! I'm so glad you called. What's up with you?"

Grey had intended this phone call to be the one where he told her about his father's accident, but instead he was calling for some information. His mother, Clare, had been hospitalized.

"Mom is in the hospital in Gustavia and I don't know what is going on with her. The doctor keeps talking about a 'CVA' and I can't get the straightforward language from them. What is that, Gretchen?" Grey's voice sounded strained and she wished she could be right there with him.

"Babe, it's a stroke. Were you there with her when it happened? " Gretchen was trying to be calm. She had to get some information from Grey since she couldn't see the chart, the vital signs, lab work, or Clare. Grey would have to paint the medical picture for her to help him understand.

"Yes. We were in the office and talking and then she got excited about something and whooped and hollered out the door. I heard her fall in the hallway. I got up to go see about her and she looked confused. She told me that she felt strange and that she had no feeling in her face or the left leg. Her left arm wouldn't work right when I tried to get her to a sitting position. I called the ambulance and they took her to the hospital. A stroke, oh Gretchen I wish you could be here with her. What should I do? What questions do I need to ask?" Grey was weary and overwhelmed.

"Honey, did they do a CT scan? If so, what did it show?" Gretchen could hear Grey asking for his mother's chart. His temper was showing. Those poor nurses would have to endure him until she could figure out a way to come.

"Where do I find that in the chart? I'm looking through it right now. It's right in front of me."

"Look for a lab or x-ray tab in her chart. Is it there?"

"Yes, do you want me to read the summary or the report?"

Grey read the summary and Gretchen was relieved. It was a clot, not a bleed that caused the stroke. It wasn't unusual for elderly to have plaque that built up in the arteries known as atherosclerosis. Sometimes those fatty deposits would break off into the bloodstream and lodge into a smaller vein causing a blockage of blood. That would hinder or completely occlude blood flow to that section of tissue and starve it from the nutrient rich blood. The tissue would atrophy or die if the blood supply wasn't restored.

In this case, the tissue affected was the brain. A blockage was much easier to treat medically than a bleed where the blood was leaking and sometimes was hard to determine its source and correct it. All this information, she relayed to Grey in layman's terms.

"Babe, this makes me feel much better to know a little more about what is going on with mom. They have been running IVs through her since she was on the ambulance. They have drawn blood and taken her to radiology. Seems they are doing everything they can. They are telling me I can see her now."

"Call me back after you've seen her. I love you." Gretchen couldn't help it. The words felt natural to say to him. She did love Grey Maddock.

There was pause on Grey's end and then, "Babe, I love you too." He quickly disconnected and went to see his mother.

Gretchen feverishly made telephone calls. She had accomplished several things by the time Grey called her back four hours later. Gretchen had managed to book herself a flight to Grey's island in the French West Indies, had arranged for Jeb to be picked up by his dad and for him to stay with him until she could get stateside again.

She was packing a suitcase when her phone rang. "Hey Babe. How's your mom doing?" Gretchen took a break and sat down to digest to what Grey was saying.

"Gretchen, she doesn't look like my mom. She is pale and weak. She is able to swallow, but her speech is slurred. She is able to move her left side a little more as time passes. Dr. Goldman says that her prognosis for recovery is good. They will be moving her soon to a rehabilitation facility. They didn't think she needed to flown to a larger hospital. She's a fighter though. The doctor said her active life would help her to recover quicker. Does this sound right to you? Do I need to be doing anything else?" Grey sounded tired and anxious.

"Grey, what the doctor has told you is encouraging. Putting her in a rehab facility will help her. They will do daily therapies that will help her get back home. I also have something else to tell you." Gretchen paused. "I have booked a flight to St. Barts to come help you with your mother."

Grey was speechless. He didn't say anything for full thirty seconds. Gretchen said, "Grey, if you don't want me to, I can cancel. I didn't mean to intrude."

"No, babe. It would mean a lot to me to have you here to help with Mom. She's been crazy to meet you." Gretchen could hear the relief in his voice and it lifted her heart.

"I've packed and will be flying out tomorrow morning at 6:15 a. m. I should be there late afternoon or so. I've rented a car so you don't have to worry about picking me up. I'll be bringing my GPS so I can find whatever I need without you having to take me anywhere. I want to be a help to you, and not be a hindrance." Gretchen was getting excited about coming to St. Barts, even though it was not on the best terms.

She planned to stay as long as she was needed. Her trainings were complete in her facilities until next May. They could reach her by phone or email while she was on the island. The corporate office was willing to give it a try for her to work out of the country.

Jeb was not happy with staying with his dad and Jean while his mother went to the Caribbean without him. He would be taken care of while she was gone. Maybe she could fly him down if the stay would need to be longer than a week or two.

Chapter Fourteen

Her flight was on time. The island used military time like she did when she charted in her nurse's notes. That might take a little adjusting to on her part.

The airport was not busy and Gretchen buzzed to the car rental desk. She picked up her keys and found her car. It was a red convertible. She didn't remember picking out a red convertible, but heck, she'd take it.

Gretchen hopped into the convertible and since the top was down she took a minute to put her curls into a ponytail. She slipped on her prize Dolce & Gabbana sights and put the pedal to the metal.

The weather was beautiful and the GPS was a Godsend. The deep manly voice told her where to turn, merge, and loop. Within about twenty minutes, she was pulling up at the hospital feeling refreshed and relaxed from her jaunt from the airport. The sun had kissed her shoulders on the drive and her freckles were popping out.

She dialed Grey's cell. " 'Lo, Babe. I'm coming out the front door of the hospital." He sounded so much better. "There's a hot babe in a red convertible out here. Maybe I should go say 'Hi!'"

"Greyson Michael Maddock. That's me." Gretchen said in a fake surly tone. She loved to have a reason to call his full name. She got out and met him. He picked her up and hugged her. And, then he kissed her. Wow.

She adjusted her shoulder bag and pushed her sunglasses up onto her head as they headed into the hospital. A dark skinned man behind the information desk addressed Grey, "Nice, mon" while he nodded and appraised Gretchen. She burst out laughing and Grey rolled his eyes and slipped a possessive arm around her waist. They walked down the hall to Clare's room.

"Mom?" Grey stuck his head in his mother's room. Grey was holding Gretchen's hand. "Mom, Gretchen's here to help take care of you, and me, too. "

Clare Maddock turned in her bed to face Gretchen. She immediately saw why Grey loved this woman. She had an open and honest face with intelligent green eyes. Gretchen was just a little shorter than Grey. Perfect fit, Clare thought and pursed her lips with a smirk. "Well, hello Gretchen. It's nice to finally meet you. Grey has said so many things about you." Although her speech was a little slurred, Gretchen understood her words perfectly.

Gretchen's face turned pink and she hoped that Ms. Maddock wouldn't notice. She really felt like she was under a microscope. "Hi, Ms. Maddock. I'm glad to meet you. I'm sorry it's under such terms. How are you feeling? Have they talked to you about your therapies?"

"Oh, pish posh, call me Clare. Come on over here and sit and tell me about yourself. I don't want to talk about therapies right now. We'll do that later. Now, we have to talk about you." Clare was motioning to Gretchen to come and sit on the edge of her bed. She walked over and sat where Clare was patting. Grey sat in the chair beside his mother's bed.

Both ladies talked until time for the evening meal about Jeb, Gretchen's flight, the sailboat business, the day Grey was born. Gretchen was afraid she was going to tire Clare out, but she was such a strong woman and she could see her potential. She knew Clare wasn't afraid to work hard. She looked forward to helping her.

Clare was doing quite well. Dr. Goldman had been in to say that the stroke was a mild one and her recovery would be much faster than he first expected. Her speech had already improved, according to Grey.

She was being fitted for a special shoe to help her keep her foot straight. It would help her gait. She was walking with a walker and she didn't like it for one minute. Gretchen would do everything she could to help Grey's mother. Helping people was her bag.

"Mom, we are going to get something to eat and we will see you in the morning. Rest well and call us if you need anything. I'll check in on you later this evening. Love you." Grey leaned and kissed his mother. Clare said goodbye to her son and Gretchen; then they were gone.

They flew down the road to Grey's house in the convertible with the top down and the sun up. Neither was all that hungry for food. They just wanted to have a drink and be alone. Now that Clare was recovering and that she felt well, the pressure had been relieved somewhat. Maybe Gretchen should have waited to come down to visit. There were the details of therapies and home health to work out with which Gretchen could help.

Pulling up to Grey's house took her breath away. His house was a beach castle. It was large, but still cozy and inviting. As they drove up the crushed shell driveway, he said to her, "You might not believe it, but you are the only woman besides my mother who has been here as an overnight guest. I hope you like it."

Gretchen stared with her eyes and jaw open. It was so great with the wooden plank porch that wrapped around the house. The blue-gray cottage castle had large windows on the back so he could see the ocean at any time and sit in the house and watch the sun set. The skylights let in the Caribbean sun without the heat. The interior had minimal furniture, but it was enough. The view out the windows was enough scenery that pictures were not needed. The faint ocean scent filled the house so that it smelled clean and fresh all the time.

The kitchen was very modern and had restaurant quality appliances. She could tell it had been used, but very well maintained. She recalled him saying he liked to cook. He had a fancy Viking stove with an indoor grill, and a retractable hood vent. Grey's backyard, which was the beach, had two Adirondack chairs and a small table in between them.

To the right side of his backyard was a small house. It was one large room with a bath off to the side. The room held a day bed, a small set of kitchen table and chairs with a Mac Book on it, a kitchenette, a couch and a TV. There were beach towels in a basket by the door. "Grey, what's the purpose of this little house? You have all that just feet away." She didn't understand.

"Gretchen, that is a nice house. But, this feels cozy for one. I spend a lot of time out here and actually lived here when I was building the cottage. It has what I need until I have a reason for more room. When I cook for friends, I use the big house's kitchen. But for sleep and day to day use, I spend my time out here." He gestured around at the tiny space. "When we would chat online, this is the table where I usually sat and there's the chair I would sit in sometimes."

"Are we sleeping here tonight?" Gretchen asked with her eyebrows raised. She considered how interesting it would be to try to both fit on the day bed or on the couch and giggled.

"No babe. We're going to sleep in the master suite in the house. I haven't shown that to you yet. I thought we would wait until later." He smiled warm and sexy at her.

They made their way back into the house and shook the sand off their feet. Grey made her a margarita, complete with salt around the rim. He fixed himself a Crown and Coke. There was nothing more satisfying than a margarita in the Caribbean.

Grey went and changed his clothes and came out in an opened buttoned-down soft green long-sleeved polo with the sleeves rolled up to reveal his strong, sun-tanned arms and a pair of loose fitting khaki cargo shorts. He was barefoot. Oh, what that man did to her. She might have to rethink the margarita being the most satisfying thing in the Caribbean. That was before she knew and loved Grey Maddock.

The tequila went straight to her head and Grey went straight to her heart. Grey made chicken quesadillas and fresh guacamole dip. They watched the sun go down from his private porch in his hot tub. At first, Gretchen thought the hot tub was the wrong thing to do in the Caribbean. After some persuasion, Grey had her convinced that nothing would be wrong in the Caribbean when she was with him.

At 9:15 p.m. he called his mom to make sure she was doing okay and didn't need anything. She assured him she was just fine. She was getting ready to go to bed and hoped he was planning to do the same. The way his mother said it made him feel embarrassed. She giggled and said, "Good night, my dear." Grey hung up and said to the phone, "Weird."

Gretchen wandered around the huge master bedroom in nothing but a towel. She couldn't believe it. It was bigger than her kitchen, dining room, breakfast nook and living room put together. Two people could lose each other in this room. That is not what she intended to happen, but it could.

Grey traipsed back in and removed her towel. "Mom's doing fine. She said she was going to bed." He kissed her and nuzzled her neck. "I think that sounds pretty good to me, too." He picked her up and carried her to the giant bed. He gently laid her on it.

Grey walked over and opened the French doors out onto his private porch, which was really private with the plants and vines placed strategically. The beach was private; so there was no chance someone would walk by and see into the house.

Grey returned to her. His timed flameless candles that his housekeeper insisted on purchasing came on at that moment. He would have to thank Concetta the next time she was here. Grey smiled and said, "This is absolutely perfect. Since we met I've wanted to make love to you in this bed with the ocean in the background." He crawled onto the bed with her.

"Oh, so you timed the candles to come on? Nice touch, lover boy. You didn't have to do all this to seduce me you know." She smiled a come hither smile and crooked a finger telling him to come to her.

"My housekeeper, Concetta, suggested it. She's a hopeless romantic, but I guess she knows what she is doing. I like the way your skin looks in the candlelight. And, when we fall asleep from exhaustive lovemaking, we won't burn down our love shack." He smiled as he kissed her.

"What do you mean by 'our' love shack?" Gretchen got a little nervous. Maybe she was just reading more into what he was saying.

"Babe, I want to marry you and I want this to be our home. Will you be Mrs. Grey Maddock?" Grey held his breath while he held her warm willing body in his bed.

"Are you serious, Grey?" Gretchen sat up in the bed, her breasts jiggling. Her curvy body easily distracted Grey. "Grey. Hellloooo?" She reached down and tipped his face up to her.

"Sorry babe. Your girls were telling me secrets. I had to listen." He grinned like a kid with his hand caught in the cookie jar. She shook her head. "Yes, I'm serious about marrying you." He leaned his head over her chest and took one of her nipples into his mouth. "I don't want to wake up and not be able to do this every morning."

Grey Maddock began a slow onslaught of love making to Gretchen Mitchell that burst a few stars in the galaxy. He made love to her with his mind, his heart, his mouth, his soul and his body. Gretchen felt thoroughly loved.

He woke her in the morning to make love to her before he took her to the office and back to the hospital to visit Clare. They shared a shower, which would have been quicker if each of them had taken their own turn. Grey grabbed bagels for them before they stopped by the office. It was just 0730 in the morning and visiting hours didn't start until 0900.

Chapter Fifteen

     Gretchen could get used to this lifestyle and being loved by Grey Maddock on a daily basis. She might even like being Mrs. Grey Maddock. She hadn't answered him last night with words but her body spoke volumes. As they pulled into the parking lot of an office building right on the pier of St. Jean's Bay, Grey said, "This is GMS, Inc. We aren't into sinking ships anymore after the job in New Orleans. We book pleasure sailing tours only." He unlocked the door and they walked into the office.

"What exactly do your pleasure tours provide, Mr. Maddock? Something I need to be worried about if I am interested in applying for the position of Mrs. Maddock?" Gretchen was trying on her best haughty face and snotty attitude. She slung her handbag onto his desk and removed her sunglasses.

Grey just grinned and stalked her around his desk. She stood with her back to him at the window. Grey came up behind her and put his arms around her waist and nibbled on her neck. "Well, for starters, Ms. Mitchell, there's not a position that I haven't had you in that you couldn't um, fill. So, there's no need to apply. However . . ." He grabbed her up and set her on his desk.

She had a surprise for Grey under her long, flowing skirt if he chose to look for it. He slid his hand up her leg while she crooked it behind his waist. It didn't take Grey Maddock long to find the treasure. He sucked in a breath, his eyes darkened, and his pants got tight. "Maybe you should be a pirate with the earring and all, Grey Maddock. You are quite effective at finding the booty even without a treasure map." She smiled and scooted to the end of his desk where he could reach her womanly treasures.

Grey and Gretchen walked into the hospital and up to Clare's room. They were hand in hand and giggling all the way up in the elevator about the broken desk. While Grey and Gretchen were feeling pretty good, the desk didn't fare so well.

"I am going to invest in some better furniture. Do you think it will be rated for making mad passionate love to a woman on it? If not, I'm not buying it." Grey was grinning while he was saying it and sliced his hand flatly through the air to make his point. Gretchen was in stitches. She was relieved to find out it wasn't an old family heirloom or antique piece.

Clare Maddock was dressed and waiting in the chair. Her suitcase was at her feet. The walker was close by and she was wearing her boot to correct her gait in her shoe. She didn't like it, but it was well camouflaged.

"Mom, what are you doing out of bed? Dr. Goldman said it would be a couple of days before you were ready to be discharged." Grey was concerned.

"Yes, well I talked to Dr. Goldman and he agreed as long as I had a nurse to oversee my therapies that I could do it from home. Isn't that great news?" Clare looked at her son and then at Gretchen.

"Mom, you can't ask that of Gretchen." Grey looked uncomfortable. He rubbed his forehead and turned to Gretchen. "Well, what do you think?"

"Clare, I want to see you walk with that walker." The nurse in Gretchen took over and Clare was no longer a potential mother-in-law, she was a patient at one of her facilities. Clare looked at her and nodded.

Clare pulled the walker around in front of her. She was a little wobbly when she stood up. The first step made Grey reach for her, but Gretchen stopped him by grabbing his arm. Clare steadied herself and stepped with the good leg first. She was getting the hang of it.

"Good, Clare." Gretchen said. She had her demonstrate some other activities of daily living. She was successful at those. Her walking without assistance was going to be the one area that needed to be worked on the most from her nursing assessment. Grey would have to take Gretchen to her house to see if it was equipped with grip bars in the tub and around the toilet and she also wanted to check the width of the doors for wheelchair access just in case. Clare was coping quite well.

Gretchen spoke with Dr. Goldman about transferring her to her own home, instead of a rehabilitation facility. The plan was made for follow up with Dr. Goldman in two weeks. Until then, Gretchen was here to help with the transition back home. Dr. Goldman gave Gretchen his cell phone number and told her to call him anytime, day or night.

Grey went to get the car and Gretchen helped Clare out to the curb. Clare said, "My son is one of the best men you will ever have in your life. I wish you all the very best. You are a keeper, honey, and I've told him that. I appreciate what you are doing for us."

"Clare, it's my job. As a nurse and as your daughter-in-law to be." Gretchen continued to look at Grey's mother. At first Clare didn't move. When the words sank in, she whooped and hollered. She hugged Gretchen's neck so tight that she nearly spilled them both into the parking lot.

From Grey's vantage point, it looked like his mother was falling and Gretchen was trying to catch her. He sped up to the curb and saw the two laughing and crying. "What's going on? I leave you two for a minute and you are falling all over the place in tears."

"I was just telling your mother that I was doing my job as a nurse and as her daughter-in-law by taking care of her." Gretchen was helping Clare into the front seat of the convertible. It was a little unconventional to be taking a stroke patient home in a convertible, but Gretchen got the feeling they were an unconventional family.

Grey nodded and said, "That's true." A moment lapsed before he looked at Gretchen. "Does this mean 'yes you will be Mrs. Grey Maddock?'" Gretchen nodded, tears filling her eyes. She was so happy. Grey ran around the car and grabbed her up. He turned circles with her in the parking lot. "You've just made me the happiest sailor in port!"

Chapter Sixteen

Grey's cell phone rang. Gretchen's voice came through the line. "Hey, Baby. Have you talked to your mom today? "

"Babe, I have and she's doing great. Felix has been out for her therapy and he was a nice man who has high hopes for mom to be walking without a walker in less than a month." Grey knew that made everyone happy. "Whatcha need Darlin'?"

"Grey, I'm having trouble with getting the Internet to connect here at the house. Do you have trouble with it?"

"I usually just connect at work or at the beach house. I haven't tried in our bedroom or in our living room or in our kitchen." He was smiling as he said it. He loved using the word 'our' when it came to Gretchen.

"I would love to come to work with you. My office can be beside yours if you have room for me. I thought I saw an empty office beside yours. Would that be too much to ask?" Gretchen was chewing on her bottom lip. She hated to be an inconvenience to him.

"Babe, great idea. I'll be home to get you in about fifteen minutes. Will you be ready?" Grey was smiling at coming home to get his woman, his wife-to-be. Usually, the interruption of needing to return home would be annoying.

"It will take me at least that long to gather up my stuff. It's strewn from one end of the house to the other." Gretchen was making a mental list until she could get to piece of paper and a pen.

"Darlin' that's not what I'm talking about."

"Oh Grey, good grief. Do you ever think of anything else? I swear your dad was Italian!" She disconnected and hurried about to gather her things. She also knew he wasn't kidding.

She was showering when he came home. They spent a fair amount of time in the shower and then she got dressed. While she was finishing getting ready, he loaded her computer, printer, and office files. She loved the detachable massager head in the master shower. All the multiple showerheads were heaven and when Grey used the massager on her, she hung from the ceiling tiles in the shower.

Gretchen had to get her head in the game again. So, once she arrived at GMS, Inc., she hooked up her Apple and went to work answering the emails. Grey was banned from her workspace until 1600. She needed no distractions. She was pleased that having a 'home office' from St Barts was working out.

Most of her facilities didn't even know she was out of the country unless she explained where she was. Her cell phone worked fine. She was waiting for the bill to come, though. She expected it to be through the roof.

She had discussed with Grey about getting a cell phone through GMS, Inc. He said that was probably going to be more efficient and just added her a phone line. The cell service company brought out a choice of new cell phones for her to choose the one she wanted. Once selected, the representative moved her address book over and simultaneous sent text and voice mail messages to the listing that her number had changed. Her old number would still call this new cell for two weeks. She felt like a phone princess.

Gretchen made her daily call to check on Jeb. Jeb answered the phone, "Mom. When you are coming home? Is Grey's mom doing okay?" Jeb was firing off the questions without waiting for her to respond.

"Jeb, slow down. " Gretchen laughed. "It's going to be a couple of weeks before I am home. Yes, Ms. Clare is doing well. She is at home and has private therapists to come to her. What's new with you? How're your dad and Jean?"

"Now, who's asking all the questions?" Jeb laughed. "Things are good here, Mom. Dad and Jean are doing fine. I want to come down there with you. Has Grey taken you sailing yet?"

Gretchen gave it some thought. "Jeb, would you like to live down here on St. Barts?" The silence stretched across the miles.

"Mom that would be way cool! Has Grey asked you to marry him yet?" Jeb sounded so brave and grown up.

"Jeb, I didn't want to tell you this over the phone, but yes, he has." Gretchen waited for her son's response.

"Whoa! That was close. I thought I had ruined the surprise." Jeb laughed nervously.

"Jeb, what are you talking about?" Gretchen was very confused.

"Mom, Grey called me a couple of weeks ago and asked if I minded if he married you. I don't know why he asked me. I told him that I didn't care as long as he taught me how to sail. Grey said it was a deal." Jeb was silent on the phone again. Then, she heard him eating something crunchy. He was very casual about the whole thing.

Gretchen felt the tears spring to her eyes. That was the time Grey picked to come into her office. He immediately was on his knee in front of her wiping away the tears that wouldn't stop coming. Now was her chance to honk into a tissue for Grey. "Mom?" Grey heard Jeb say.

Grey took the phone from Gretchen and he said, "Hey Dude, it's Grey. Your mom is crying. Wanna tell me what's going on?"

"Oh man, girls are just like water faucets! I told her you called me to ask if you could marry her. Did she say no or something?" Jeb stopped chewing and was now worried about his mom.

Grey chuckled. "Hey, I gotcha. Nope, she's good. The tears are happy ones. She said yes. It will take you about 42 years to learn all the wonderful things about girls, my man. I'll teach you a little bit about what I know. I'll have your mom call you tomorrow, okay kiddo?" Grey and Jeb disconnected.

By then, Gretchen had it under control again and she said, "I have to approve what things you teach my son about girls. He is only ten, you know." The love was showing through her watery smile. "It was so sweet that you asked my son if you could marry his mother. I appreciate you involving him in us like you do."

"Jeb is going to be my family, too. You and your son are a package deal, Babe. I have something for you. C'mon. Bring the tissues." Grey helped her close up her office and they took off for the docks, their arms around each other.

The *Perserverance* was waiting to be boarded. It was Grey's private sailboat. Once Grey and Gretchen boarded and the crew had the table set, they stepped off and wished them a good night. She felt underdressed for the fancy works on the boat. "We aren't going out to spear fish, are we?" Gretchen was curious about the formality.

"No, not tonight. But I do have something just as awesome in mind. Right now, I'm going to give you a foot massage, a glass of red wine and I am going to feed you." Grey started working on her feet and she started on a bottle of red wine. Next, he began getting finger food out of the kitchen and placing it before her on the table. Between the red wine and the foot massage, she was barely breathing. When he set her plate in front of her, there was a blue square box on it.

"How am I supposed to eat this? Is there some sauce to dip it in or what?" She smiled and thought she probably looked goofy at her attempt at humor.

"Babe. Just open it." Grey watched with anticipation as she opened the box. It gave a little creak and Gretchen squealed with delight.

She was looking at a very large emerald in a platinum setting. "Grey, that's the biggest thing I've ever seen!" She was grinning from ear to ear.

Grey moved to sit beside her on the deck. "Yeah, I get that reaction a lot." He gave her the lopsided grin she'd grown to love and find so sexy on his handsome face.

Despite his sex appeal, she elbowed him. "You better not use that line or anything else you have on anyone but me. You are mine. " She smiled, kissed his lips and put the 'so large it can't be real' emerald solitaire ring on her ring finger of her left hand.

"Let me tell you about this ring. I've had this ring for about three months now. I knew when I saw it in Tiffany that it belonged on your finger. It is 6.3 karats of princess cut emerald set in platinum. There is a beautiful eternity band that matches it with emerald and diamonds that alternate. If you don't like that as your wedding set, then we will shop for another, but I wanted you to have this ring. I love you." Grey put his arms around her and kissed her.

Since Grey, Gretchen had been wooed, screwed and tattooed and it was freaking fabulous! The wine must have gone to her head because she thought she might have said those elegant words to her fiancée while he packed her glorious butt to the bedroom. "You had too much to drink to remember anything that happens in our bedroom tonight." Grey laughed and tucked her in and crawled in beside her.

Gretchen woke in the morning and heard Grey in the shower. She couldn't resist joining him. They were becoming more efficient with the morning sex-in-the-shower routine. And, they were getting faster at getting ready for work together.

Gretchen was at her desk answering emails for work and from her friends, too. Once she had established the Internet connection, she had kept Lou and Cherie in the loop of what was going on her life. Lou of course said, "I told you so. Glad you went for it." Cherie wanted to know when they could come down and see her. She had not told them the news that she was getting married.

Clare was getting better every day. She had switched gears from planning a huge Christmas celebration to planning a huge Christmas wedding celebration. All this planning made Clare very happy and so Gretchen allowed her to do it. She was walking several feet without her walker. Gretchen was so proud of her achievement.

Grey, in his spare time, had gathered some information about the private school down the road from GMS, Inc. Their academics were superior to stateside schooling as far as ACT/SAT scores. They had soccer and basketball as options for two sports. The only thing Jeb would be missing would be scouting and his dad. Gretchen was thankful that Grey had checked into schooling for Jeb. It was very much a 'step-dad' thing to do.

It was time to make a trip to Missouri and she needed two tickets. Grey was going with her since his mother was doing so well. Hopefully, Jeb was coming back with her permanently. There were some details to work out with Jake.

She packed a suitcase for both of them. It felt intimate that their clothes touched in the luggage. Gretchen felt so giddy about it and also felt very blessed to have found such a wonderful man.

It was working out well to have her office in Grey's business building. The Internet connection was strong and reliable. The new cell phones were working out beautifully. Her facilities were able to reach her without difficulty. Gretchen even had a phone conference with the corporate office.

Grey was looking forward to helping Gretchen tie up any loose ends in Missouri. The faster they got that done, the faster they would be back at home in the Caribbean with Jeb. He had to find a way to tell her about the accident with his dad.

Grey knew after talking with his mother that his worth as a man wasn't defined by that moment, but all moments of his life. He came to the realization that it wasn't his fault and his dad wouldn't want him to blame himself. He would feel much better once Gretchen knew the truth about that day.

On the drive from St. Louis to Gretchen's yellow house, Grey reached over and took Gretchen's hand. Gretchen looked up from her book and said, "What is it, Grey?" She could tell that he needed to tell her something.

Gretchen became alarmed when Grey pulled over at a small rest area. He put the car in park and turned to her. "Gretchen, I want to tell you something. Remember when I was vague about my father's accident?" She nodded and squeezed his hand in encouragement. "He was coming out to rescue me."   Grey relayed the rest of the story to Gretchen, stopping two times to get his emotions under control. He explained to her that he, at one time, felt responsible. Grey said, "I was afraid if I said it out loud, then it would be true that I killed my father. I was more afraid of you leaving when you knew the truth about my selfishness."

Gretchen hurt for the man she loved. She wanted a way to take away his pain, but kissed his tears away instead. She said to him, "Grey, you are not a selfish man. Knowing about your father's accident wouldn't change my mind about you. You are so much more than one moment in time. I don't mean to sound cliché, but bad things happen to good people. I love you and nothing will change that."

Grey was very relieved to hear those words from Gretchen. "Oh babe, I love you, too. What would I do without you? You are so smart and caring and everything I want in a woman."

Gretchen smiled at him and kissed him on the nose. "Without me, you would be spending lots of cold nights alone. Now, put this car in gear and let's get to the house. I'm ready to get packed up so we can get back home."

Home. Grey thought that sounded pretty good. Especially knowing that Gretchen would be there, too.

Chapter Seventeen

As Grey pulled into the driveway of the cake mix yellow house, Gretchen didn't have a sense of this being home anymore. She missed Jeb, but not Missouri. She had decided wherever Grey was, that was home. She opened the door to the house and stepped inside.

Jeb was there in the living room. He had a packed suitcase at his feet. "Jeb, what are you doing, son?" Gretchen walked in to hug her son's neck.

"I don't want you to go without me again. I knew what time your flight got in and I wanted to be ready." Jeb was very glad to see both of them. He even hugged Grey.

Gretchen explained that she would have to work some things out with his father and check with the school about transferring his school credits. He handed Gretchen a package. It was full of all of his credits. His counselor had helped him look up everything about the private school down the road from GMS, Inc. She had mentioned the private school, but Jeb must have been paying more attention than she thought. It seemed that everything he would need for school information was in the packet. Now, just to talk to Jeb's dad.

"Mom, I talked to dad and I think he'll be okay with me moving down there with you and Grey. He did want you to call him." Gretchen shook her head. He was the man of the house. "Of course I'm going to talk to your dad. You don't think I'd just take a ten-year-old's word for it? Especially when that ten-year-old wants to learn how to sail." She smirked and crooked her arm around Jeb's neck. Grey just smiled and asked her what she wanted to take back besides her son.

While Grey and Jeb made light work of packing the things that were going to St. Barts, Gretchen went to talk to Jake and Jean. Gretchen explained the plan for Jeb to return to the island with her. He would be enrolled in the school down the road from the GMS, Inc. Her nurse consulting office was also in the building. Jake and Jean would be given tickets twice a year through the shipping company to see Jeb. Jeb could fly back to Missouri anytime he wanted to see his dad and Poppa Bill.

The child support payments would go into an annuity for Jeb that Jake would control from home. Father and son would decide how that money was to be spent. That was Jake's idea.

Jake had talked with his lawyer and had the papers drafted. He thought it sounded fair and thought that Gretchen would also be in agreement. Jake had made an appointment for tomorrow afternoon if that worked for her. Gretchen agreed to meet him there to sign. The only words out of Jean Mitchell's mouth during the whole conversation between Jake and Gretchen were, "That is the biggest emerald I've ever seen! Is it real?"

Gretchen called Lou and Cherie for an emergency Margarita meeting. Grey and Jeb went for pizza and putt

putt golf and a movie if they cruised by and the ladies' cars were still in the driveway.

Her friends came out and Gretchen had already had a couple of margaritas. They always went down so easily, especially with good company.

Lou said, "OK, spill it. I want to hear all the details of this man that has rocked your world!"

"Yes, details, details!" Cherie screamed and then licked some salt off the rim of the glass.

"Well, you know I am faulting the two of you for this. If I hadn't been in New Orleans with the two of you, I would have never hooked up with Greyson Maddock, Jr. He's a wonderful man and a clever lover. I don't think I will grow tired of him anytime soon." Gretchen stopped to dramatically fan herself and then laughed with the girls. "Now for something a little more serious. I am going to become Mrs. Greyson Maddock, Jr. on December 19th and I have four tickets for you and the men in your life." The ladies screamed and cried and jumped up and down and hugged and almost fell over the packed up boxes. They ooed and aahed over Gretchen's emerald ring and her new-found life.

On the radio, Garth Brooks began to sing, "I've got friends in low places..." Gretchen realized that if she had not had her friends, she would be in a low place. Gretchen's life turned out to be full of wonderful surprises.

The three best friends laughed, drank and sang along with Garth Brooks. They finished off the first pitcher. As an encore, the blender whirred to life.

The End!

Thank you for reading! You can reach me at
boyer_farms@yahoo.com. I am writing a second
book, which is very different from this one.
I like reading and writing different genres.

www.ingramcontent.com/pod-product-compliance
Lightning Source LLC
Chambersburg PA
CBHW071327130626
46556CB00004B/1785